THE PERILS OF LOVE

The Perils of Love

LEFT BEHIND

>THE KIDS<

Jerry B. Jenkins

Tim LaHaye

WITH CHRIS FABRY

TYNDALE
KIDS

TYNDALE HOUSE PUBLISHERS, INC.
WHEATON, ILLINOIS

Visit Tyndale's exciting Web site at www.tyndale.com

Discover the latest Left Behind news at www.leftbehind.com

Published in association with the literary agency of Alive Communications, Inc., 7680 Goddard Street, Suite 200, Colorado Springs, CO 80920.

Edited by Lorie Popp

ISBN 0-8423-8348-4, mass paper

Printed in the United States of America

08 07 06 05 04
8   7   6   5   4   3   2   1

To Mallory Kessel

TABLE OF CONTENTS

What's Gone On Before xi

1. Trapped in New Babylon 1

2. Rainer 13

3. Attack 27

4. Rainer's Sacrifice 37

5. Captured 49

6. Judd's New Mission 61

7. Zvi 73

8. The Blind See 85

9. The Meeting 97

10. The Island 109

11. Bad News in San Diego 121

12. The Missing Mark 133

13. Otto Weser 143

14. The World Watches 155

15. Last Words 167

16. Holding Kenny 181

About the Authors

THE YOUNG TRIBULATION FORCE

Original members—Vicki Byrne, Judd Thompson, Lionel Washington

Other members—Mark, Conrad, Darrion, Janie, Charlie, Shelly, Melinda

OTHER BELIEVERS

Chang Wong—Chinese teenager working in New Babylon

Tsion Ben-Judah—Jewish scholar who writes about prophecy

Colin and Becky Dial—Wisconsin couple

Sam Goldberg—Jewish teenager, Lionel's good friend

Mr. Mitchell Stein—Jewish friend of the Young Trib Force

Naomi Tiberius—computer whiz living in Petra

Chaim Rosenzweig—famous Israeli scientist

Zeke Zuckermandel—disguise specialist for the Tribulation Force

Marshall Jameson—leader of the Avery, Wisconsin, believers

UNBELIEVERS

Nicolae Carpathia—leader of the Global Community

Leon Fortunato—Carpathia's right-hand man

What's Gone On Before

JUDD Thompson Jr. and his friends in the Young Tribulation Force are living the adventure of a lifetime. Nearing the six-year mark of the Tribulation, a heat wave devastates the world. Believers are able to move around freely during the day, so Judd and Lionel drive to Wisconsin to join their friends.

After a tearful reunion and a welcome-home party, Judd and Vicki decide to help move people and supplies around the country. When they discover a member of an Ohio group missing, Judd and Vicki help their new friend Howard escape.

As the heat wave continues, Judd and Vicki grow closer. On an isolated road in Wisconsin, Judd proposes marriage and Vicki accepts. They ask Dr. Tsion Ben-Judah if he will perform the ceremony, and Tsion suggests they relocate to Petra.

Judd accompanies pilot Westin Jakes on a supply run to New Babylon. There, they stay overnight with a group of believers living right under Nicolae Carpathia's nose.

The next morning, Judd calls Chang Wong at the palace in New Babylon. Chang says the heat wave is over, and Judd's heart sinks. He's thousands of miles from Vicki in the most hostile location on the planet.

Join the Young Tribulation Force as they struggle to survive during the last year of the Great Tribulation.

ONE

Trapped in New Babylon

JUDD Thompson Jr. fell into a chair and gasped for breath. It felt like the air had been sucked out of his lungs. He couldn't believe he was trapped in New Babylon, the headquarters of the Global Community.

Judd spoke with Chang Wong for a few more minutes, and Chang said he would call with any information that might help Judd and pilot Westin Jakes escape.

Then Judd joined the others gathered around several computers. Some monitored cameras set up near their safe house, while others watched the latest from the Global Community News Network.

Rainer Kurtzmann, the German leader of this small group, took Judd aside. "I'm sorry you're trapped. I feel responsible for not getting you back to your plane last night."

Judd frowned. "It's not your fault. Westin and I made a bad choice."

"Whatever we can do to help, we will do."

A woman pointed to a tiny laptop computer. "Take a look at this."

Judd watched as a temperature gauge on the right side showed things were back to normal. The woman moved a remote camera slightly to the left, and several people crawled out of an underground bunker. Their skin was pale, and they looked like they hadn't eaten in weeks.

The woman zoomed in on a smiling group. A young man ran to a burned-out area and lay down, scissor-kicking as if making a snow angel. The others with him laughed.

The mood inside the safe house wasn't cheerful. They would no longer be able to move around during the day. Westin grumbled about his plane, wondering if the GC would find it.

"We have to prepare for possible inspections by Peacekeepers," Rainer said. "They'll be going from building to building soon."

A live shot of Carpathia's palace showed open windows and people streaming out of the building. Judd wondered if the GC would ever estimate how many had died from the heat.

Leon Fortunato appeared at a press conference, and Judd was shocked at the way the reporters looked. The normal crowd of men and women covering international news was down to only a few people in ragged clothes. Even makeup couldn't hide their gaunt faces.

Fortunato was dressed in his usual gaudy clothing, but Judd could tell the past few weeks had taken their toll. There were dark circles under Leon's eyes, and his clothes seemed to sag.

"I'm pleased to say that your potentate will speak just before noon today to give an update on the world situation," Fortunato said. "But I am happy to report that it appears this quirk of nature is over. We have reports from everywhere the sun is up that the heat is gone. Let us give thanks to the giver of all good things, Nicolae Carpathia."

Vicki awoke with a gasp and sat up in bed. The rhythmic breathing of the others in the cabin calmed her, but something didn't feel right. She listened for any noise outside but heard nothing. The heat wave had done many things to help believers, even zapping insects. Rivers and lakes had boiled for so long that frogs were nonexistent. Crickets, cicadas, and other bugs had either gone into hiding or had been burned to a crisp. Vicki was glad she could go out during the day because walking at night was so quiet it was eerie.

Vicki had awakened at other times and sensed a need to pray for friends. Perhaps this was such a time. Could someone be in trouble? Judd?

She closed her eyes and lay back on the pillow, whispering a prayer. Vicki found it better to pray aloud because when she prayed silently, she got distracted and sometimes simply fell asleep.

When Vicki had first become a believer, prayer had seemed like a duty. She ticked off a list of things she needed God to do, made sure she confessed her sins, got in the right amount of praise and worship, and went on with her life. But it had been six years now, and her view of prayer had changed. Just like she looked forward to talking with Judd and spending time with him, she looked forward to her times alone with God. In fact, speaking with her heavenly Father didn't feel stiff and formal—it felt natural.

Vicki discovered what had been missing from her prayer life a few years earlier: listening. She had always thought that prayer meant *saying* things *to* God. Now she remained silent for a few minutes, letting God bring back passages she had memorized or bits of verses.

At first, she had been unsure of how to address God. Should she talk to Jesus, call out to God, Father, heavenly Father, or say something else? She finally realized that God was more concerned with her simply coming to him, but she had found calling him "Father" a comforting way to begin.

"Father," Vicki prayed, "I don't know if something is wrong or if I'm up because of something I ate, but I want to listen now. I pray for Judd and the plans he has for the wedding and where we'll live once I get to Petra. Keep him safe, Father. . . ."

Vicki paused, suddenly thinking of a verse Marshall had quoted a few days before. The words she recalled were *perfect peace*, but she couldn't think of the rest. She flipped on a flashlight and grabbed her Bible from the floor. Shelly said something in her sleep and rolled over in the bed next to Vicki's.

Vicki remembered the passage was from Isaiah and turned to chapter 26, the one Marshall had been speaking about. She found her answer in the third verse.

You will keep in perfect peace all
who trust in you,
whose thoughts are fixed on you!

Is God telling me something? Vicki thought.
Is something about to happen?
She continued reading the passage.

Trust in the Lord always, for the Lord God
is the eternal Rock.
He humbles the proud and brings the
arrogant city to the dust.
Its walls come crashing down!
The poor and oppressed trample it under-
foot.
But for those who are righteous, the path
is not steep and rough. You are a God of
justice, and you smooth out the road ahead
of them.
Lord, we love to obey your laws; our
heart's desire is to glorify your name.
All night long I search for you; earnestly
I seek for God. For only when you come to
judge the earth will people turn from wick-
edness and do what is right.
Your kindness to the wicked does not
make them do good. They keep doing wrong
and take no notice of the Lord's majesty.
O Lord, they do not listen when you
threaten. They do not see your upraised fist.

Show them your eagerness to defend your people. Perhaps then they will be ashamed. Let your fire consume your enemies.

Lord, you will grant us peace, for all we have accomplished is really from you.

Vicki shook her head at the timeless words. She couldn't wait to meet the writers of the Bible and hear what they had been going through when they penned words like these. She smiled as she read the end of the twelfth verse again: *". . . for all we have accomplished is really from you."*

Footsteps sounded on the path outside. Vicki switched off the flashlight and sat up in bed. The door creaked open, and Vicki's heart pounded as she squinted to see who was coming.

"Vicki?" Mark whispered. "You awake?"

"Yeah," Vicki said, leaning back on her pillow. She knew Mark had been on duty in the main cabin keeping watch for the night.

"Better come with me," Mark said.

Vicki was dressed in seconds and ran up the path, catching up to Mark just before he entered the main cabin.

"What is it?" Vicki said.

"Phone call. Bad news."

Judd waited for Vicki to come to the phone, visualizing the cabins she would pass. He cringed when she answered, sounding out of breath and worried.

"I'm sorry to call so late," Judd said. "I wanted you to hear this from me instead of something over GCNN."

"What's wrong?"

Judd told her the heat wave had lifted in New Babylon and that it was expected to do the same throughout the world. Vicki gasped when Judd told her where he was.

"What are you going to do?" Vicki said.

"We're keeping a watch on the place until sundown. Westin and I are hoping to make it back to the plane and head for Petra."

Vicki paused, and Judd thought she was crying. Instead, Vicki shared a verse she had just looked up and told Judd to read it as well.

"You're not mad at me?" Judd said.

"I'm terrified the GC will find you and I'll see you on some newscast. But we've been through this before."

"I'll let you know as soon as anything changes," Judd said.

The two prayed and this time Vicki did cry.

When he hung up, he went to the computer and composed an e-mail, telling

Vicki all the things he couldn't say over the phone. He marked the message "private" and sent it.

As promised, Nicolae Carpathia addressed the world from the rooftop of the palace. For some reason God had spared the building. Judd noticed someone had set up fake plants and trees behind Nicolae to make it look like things were back to normal. A well-placed group of smiling GC workers stood behind him, as if the deaths of millions around the world meant nothing.

Nicolae beamed as he strutted toward the microphone. His hair fluffed in the wind. "As we prepare to partake of our noonday meal here in New Babylon, it is a festive atmosphere. We are all celebrating the end of the curious heat wave that enveloped the planet, and we look forward to the days ahead where we expect peace to rain down on us like a waterfall.

"For those who are in time zones where the sun has not yet risen, rest assured that I have taken care of this problem, with the help of my scientists, who have been working around the clock."

"Right," Rainer said. "Nicolae has been able to stop the heat wave with his injured little mind."

"The heating of the earth has actually caused the waterways to heal themselves, but there is more work to do," Carpathia said. "Those who are without homes will see them constructed in the quickest manner possible.

"In the past when we have faced hardships, we have pulled together as a Global Community, and that is what will happen now. Let us use this trouble to unite our hearts and minds for one common goal of peace. And let the enemies of peace beware, for we are more committed than ever to reaching our goal."

With his eyes flashing, Nicolae spoke in several different languages, telling people of the world that he was in control and that he had plans for the good of every person alive.

Hours later, Chang Wong phoned Judd and played part of a conversation Chang had recorded. "This is Nicolae behind closed doors with all of his top people. They spent most of the day just trying to settle people in their offices, but once the directors were there . . . well, listen."

Judd heard Nicolae rub his hands together as he said, "For the first time in a long time, we play on an even field. The waterways are healing themselves, and we have rebuilding to do in the infrastructure. Let us work at getting all our loyal citizens back onto the same page with us. Director Akbar and I have some special surprises in store for dissidents on various levels. We are back in business, people. It is time to recoup our losses and start delivering a few."

"What does that mean?" Judd said.

"I'm not sure, but I'd bet the GC knows something about what we've been doing the last few weeks, moving supplies and people. They want to hurt us."

"Anything new from the Trib Force?" Judd said.

"Everybody's back in hiding. Captain Steele says we have to pick our spots and strategize for the new night schedule. Which brings me to my other news."

"What's that?"

"Westin's plane."

Judd took a breath. "You think it's safe for us to make a run for it after dark?"

"I wish I had better news. I tapped into one of the local security channels a little earlier. The GC spotted the plane and some-how pulled it near one of the burned-out hangars at the airfield."

"So we might have to fight them to get it back?"

"No. All the fighting in the world won't

help. They planted a bomb on board thinking it was a Judah-ite aircraft."

Judd clenched his teeth. "So we'll have to
disarm—"

"Judd, listen—"

"No, Chang. If Westin and I can get to the
plane tonight and get in the air, won't God
protect us like he has protected all the other
planes?"

"Judd, something went wrong with the
detonator. The bomb exploded. There is no
plane left to fly."

Two

Rainer

WHEN Judd told Westin about the plane, Westin cursed and slammed a fist on the table. "Forgive me," he said. "This whole thing is so messed up."

"It's understandable," Rainer said. "You wouldn't be human if you didn't show emotion about this."

Westin stroked a few days' growth of beard. "I guess I should be glad the plague didn't end while we were on our way to the plane." He glanced at Judd. "Guess your wedding plans are on hold."

"We're going to get out of here," Judd said.

Rainer nodded. "We're all hoping that's true because of the prophecy."

"What prophecy?" Judd said.

Rainer took a Bible from the middle of the table. "We came here to fight the GC and live right under Carpathia's nose. But the Bible motivated us."

"What's the Bible got to do with it?" Westin said.

"One of my friends—at least he used to be a friend—was studying the book of Revelation one day and came across an interesting verse."

Rainer flipped toward the end of the Bible and found chapter 18 and began reading. " 'After all this I saw another angel come down from heaven with great authority, and the earth grew bright with his splendor. He gave a mighty shout, "Babylon is fallen—that great city is fallen! She has become the hideout of demons and evil spirits, a nest for filthy buzzards, and a den for dreadful beasts." ' "

"Filthy buzzards, dreadful beasts, that's the New Babylon I know," Westin said.

"Here's where things get interesting," Rainer said. " 'Then I heard another voice calling from heaven, "Come away from her, my people. Do not take part in her sins, or you will be punished with her. For her sins are piled as high as heaven, and God is ready to judge her for her evil deeds. Do to her as she has done to your people. Give her a double penalty for all her evil deeds. She brewed a cup of terror for others, so give her twice as much as she gave out. She has lived in luxury and pleasure, so match it now with torments and sorrows. She boasts, 'I am queen on my throne. I am no helpless widow. I will not experience sorrow.' Therefore, the sorrows of death and mourning and famine will overtake her in a single day. She will be utterly consumed by fire, for the Lord God who judges her is mighty.' "

"I don't get it," Westin said. "I mean, I understand the city is going to be destroyed by God, but why would that make you want to come here?"

Rainer smiled. "When it says, 'Come away from her, my people,' we believe that means there will be true followers of God right in New Babylon. We couldn't imagine who they would be, and then God placed a desire on our hearts to come here and either *join* this band of brave fighters or *become* a part of the biblical history."

"How many of you came?" Judd said.

"There were thirty-eight altogether," Rainer said.

Judd had asked Rainer earlier if any members of his group had been killed. Rainer hadn't wanted to talk about it.

"Those verses beg some questions," Westin said. "If God's people are supposed to come out, how are they supposed to do it, and where do they go?"

Rainer nodded. "I have been thinking about that. It's clear God has had enough of the lies and killing of New Babylon, so he's going to destroy this evil city. But there must be something coming that will signal that it's time for us to leave. That's what we've been waiting for."

"Is it possible to talk with someone else?" Judd said. "What's the leader's name again?"

"You mean Otto Weser?"

"Yeah, he might have some ideas."

Rainer pursed his lips. "We have had no contact since . . . for quite a while. It's one of our unwritten rules. No one talks with Otto."

Judd glanced at Westin. There was something behind this Otto business, and Judd wanted to find out what it was.

☀

Vicki and a few others had gone outside to watch the sun rise early the next morning. As it peeked over the hills in the distance, Vicki could tell the heat and humidity were gone, along with most of the smoke that had hovered over the valley.

At noon, Vicki ventured to the knoll above the campground. There was a lot of excitement with the weather change, more news from the Global Community, and activity on

the kids' Web site. But the news of Judd
made Vicki want to be alone.

It was spring, and the trees in the distance
should have been covered with buds and
new leaves. Instead, the countryside looked
like some burned scar.

Something skittered along the ground and
startled her. A half-burned tail flicked back
and forth on the side of a tree. A squirrel.
How he had survived the heat and fires, Vicki
didn't know, but here he was, scampering up
a tree with his charred tail.

"How many friends have you lost in the
last few years, little fella?" Vicki whispered.
She brought her knees up to her chest. She
and her friends were like this squirrel, forag-
ing, darting into hiding places, hoping to
stay alive just one more day.

Vicki recalled the verse about God knowing even when a sparrow fell from the sky.
But did God know every squirrel, raccoon,
and deer that died in the heat plague? Did he
see the death and devastation and hear the
cries of believers who had been killed?
Already the Global Community News
Network reported arrests and beheadings.

Will Judd be next?

Vicki knew it was against the group's rules
to be outside at this time of day, so she stood

and started for her cabin. Something was bothering her, and she couldn't put a finger on it.

She paused near a burned tree and heard movement at the bottom of the knoll. Someone was coming up the hill.

※

A few minutes later Judd found Rainer sitting alone in a room set aside for prayer. Several chairs sat in an empty circle, and Judd took one directly across from the German. Someone had painted a man kneeling in prayer on the wall. On the opposite wall was a painting, torn and weathered, of an old man with a piece of bread in front of him. The old man's hands were folded, and his eyes were shut tightly. Judd thought the picture looked familiar, then realized it was the same one that hung in his grandparents' kitchen.

Rainer looked up, his eyes cloudy. "I suppose you want to know what happened between Otto and me."

Judd nodded. "You don't have to tell me, but it might help me understand."

Rainer put his head back and closed his eyes. His face was strong and handsome, and his hair reached his shoulders. Judd knew he had been an actor in Germany, but what kind?

With his eyes still closed, Rainer spoke. "When light and dark collide and ignorance takes up the sword against understanding, what is left for weary men to do?" He paused, opened his eyes. "We, the weary, pick up pieces from the battlefield and live."

"What's that from?" Judd said.

"A play I was writing at the time of the disappearances. It wasn't very good."

"Sounded good to me."

Rainer smiled. "Do you know what an understudy is?"

"A person who's there in case the lead gets sick?"

"Yes. Before the vanishings, I was just an understudy at life. I knew all the lines and where to move and what to do onstage, but I was watching from behind some curtain. It took the most terrible situation in the world to bring me out of the shadows."

"You're talking about your relationship with God, right?"

Rainer nodded.

"Had you heard about God before the disappearances?"

"Many times. I had an aunt who told my brothers and sisters and me Bible stories. She was very dramatic. I think it was because of her that I wanted to become an actor."

"Were your parents believers?"

"No. They were killed in the earthquake. On a cruise down the Rhine River, the ship capsized and all but a few drowned."

"I'm sorry."

Rainer sighed. "So am I. I went to my aunt's house not long after she disappeared and relived some of those stories she used to tell. I still have her Bible. But I didn't make my decision to follow God until I stumbled onto Tsion Ben-Judah's Web site. My wife and I prayed the night after we discovered it."

"And your wife is back in Germany?"

Rainer closed his eyes. "No, she is waiting for me on the other side. Sometimes I dream that Gretchen and I are together on a beach somewhere. Talking. Laughing. Then I wake up and face this." He put his head in his hands. "I wish I could go back and talk to the people we were before the disappearances. I would convince us of the truth before any of this happened."

Rainer looked at Judd with tears in his eyes. "Sometimes I wonder if I'm here in New Babylon because it's God's will for me, or if I'm on a mission of death. One mistake and I'd be reunited with my wife forever."

"What happened to her?" Judd said.

Vicki moved behind the tree and watched as Lionel made his way toward the knoll. She thought about jumping out and scaring him but decided against it.

"Marshall sent me up here to see about you," Lionel said when he had caught his breath. "You okay?"

Vicki asked Lionel to sit. "I was up here thinking. I like this place. I'm going to miss it when I go to Petra."

Lionel bit his lower lip. "Vicki, I've always appreciated what a friend you've been, and I couldn't be happier for you and Judd . . ."

"But what?"

Lionel shook his head. "I don't know. Maybe God's trying to tell you something. Maybe you shouldn't go to Petra. Maybe Judd shouldn't have gone to New Babylon." Vicki slipped an arm around Lionel, and the young man hung his head. "He's the best friend I've ever had. I just wish he would be more careful."

Vicki looked at the sky. It had been weeks since she had seen any real clouds. Now some dark ones moved in and threatened rain. "I've been thinking a lot about what happens after the Glorious Appearing," she said. "Wondering if we'll know each other, if people will get married. If those who were married before the Rapture will be reunited."

"And what about people like Captain Steele?" Lionel said. "He was married to Mrs. Steele and then married Amanda. What about that?"

"I've been looking at Scripture, but I can't figure it out. There's got to be an answer."

"Why not go right to the top?" Lionel stood. "Let's get back. You can write Dr. Ben-Judah."

Judd listened as Rainer's story unfolded. The man described how he had met Otto Weser at a secret Bible study. Their first fight with Global Community forces had been in Stuttgart. It was Otto's idea to come into the heart of Carpathia territory, and thirty-seven others had followed.

"Otto is a verbose man. He rattles on and on. Well, we finally found a way to fly into the desert and take a slow route in separate vehicles. Otto didn't like it. He thought we should all go together, pretending to be GC recruits. There was such a disagreement that many split from the group. About a dozen decided to go a different way."

"And you went with Otto?" Judd said.

"Yes. Everything seemed fine during the trip. Our plane landed, and we bought an old school bus and started the journey across the desert. Otto was sure God was leading us. We huddled in the back of the bus, praying. My wife and I broke away from the others at one point and had our own prayer time."

Rainer pulled out his wallet and opened to a picture of a woman with long, dark hair. She looked like a famous actress Judd had seen. "She's very beautiful."

"Yes, she was." Rainer folded his wallet and put it away. "We were carrying some sophisticated heat weapons, along with machine guns and old AK-47s. It was our plan, if we were stopped, to take out any GC force before they could report us.

"We came to an unexpected checkpoint, a surprise from the Global Community. Before we could react, several Peacekeepers had surrounded the bus. We took our positions as Otto got out. We fired all of the heat weapons and the Peacekeepers rolled on the ground, but one of them managed to lob a grenade at the back of the bus. If we had seen it, we would have been able to react, but no one did."

"And the explosion killed your wife?" Judd said.

"It was a chest wound. She was in much pain. She said that I should carry on the fight without her. The last thing she said was that she would be waiting for me on the other side."

Judd sat back and shook his head. He couldn't imagine the man's pain at seeing his wife die. "How many died?"

"My brother, his best friend, and the man's wife were killed in the attack. There was no time to bury them. We simply took the GC squad cars and split up."

"What about the other group?"

"They made it with no problems," Rainer said.

"Did you ever talk with Otto about what happened?"

"I was so angry that I couldn't. I said I would never speak to him again." Rainer put his elbows on his knees and leaned forward. "This is why I say I might be on a mission of death. It is better for me to leave this place than stay."

"You really think your wife would want you to do that?"

Rainer smiled. "She was such a tough lady." He slapped his knees and stood. "I'll tell you my new mission. To get you and this Vicki girl of yours back togeth—"

One of the other members of the group rushed into the room. "It's the GC. They're on this block and headed our way. House to house."

THREE

Attack

JUDD watched the people in the hideout go into crisis mode. He and Westin stood back as the group sealed doors and tried to make it impossible for the GC to enter.

"They've placed booby traps around the house, but they're not activated yet," Westin said.

"What kind of booby traps?"

"Explosives. Mines."

"We need everyone quiet and in your places," Rainer called. "Judd, you and Westin come with me."

In the lowest point of the basement was a row of computers and machines. The chief technical person, a woman Judd knew only as Helga, manipulated a mechanical arm on the first floor. With a few quick movements she pushed some charred debris over the trapdoor, pulled a tarp over the whole mess, and made the mechanical arm disappear into the floor.

A silence fell over the room as the monitor showed a GC squad car making its way down the street. Peacekeepers carrying rifles followed.

"Are they looking for bodies?" Judd whispered.

"With rifles?" Rainer said. "They may find bodies in the rubble around here, but they're looking for anyone alive without the mark of Carpathia."

The squad car finally pulled in front of the safe house, and several Peacekeepers approached.

Helga turned to Rainer, who was scribbling something on paper. "Wait for my signal."

The Peacekeepers knocked on the sides of the house and called out. A Peacekeeper walked up to the porch and banged the door.

Judd could feel his heart beating as he watched. The room grew hotter with all the bodies and equipment.

Judd had felt unnerved by Rainer and the others talking about war and killing. There was quite a difference in being against the Global Community—escaping from them and fighting for the souls of people who had not yet taken the mark—and actually killing Carpathia followers. On the other hand, God was going to judge evil. Judd wanted to hear what Tribulation Force leaders would say. Would they actually shoot to kill and be a part of the final battle?

Judd noticed a panel filled with buttons and knobs. Underneath each was a piece of tape with writing. Judd pointed to it and Westin leaned over. "Helga told me those activate the bombs. And those over there are for guns hidden in a burned-out part of the roof."

"They can actually shoot by remote control?"

Westin nodded. "But once we start shooting, we give away our position. The GC can come in and wipe us out."

Rainer pushed his way through the gathering and into the hall. He paused when he came to Judd and handed him an envelope. "Take this."

Nothing was written on the envelope. Judd shoved it in his pocket.

Rainer tapped another man on the shoulder and they were gone.

"Is there any other way out of here?" Judd said to Westin.

Westin shrugged.

A man beside him leaned over. "There is an air lock on the other side of the basement that leads into the sewers. That's only to be used as a last resort."

"There are more officers coming," Helga said, looking around. "Where's Rainer?"

A buzzer pierced the small room, and a red light blinked on the computer.

Helga turned the alarm off. "The air lock is open. Someone's going outside."

Rainer, Judd thought.

Several men rushed out of the room. Judd kept his eyes on the monitor showing the roving Peacekeepers. They poked and prodded through the rubble above. One man pulled the tarp back and noticed the scattered debris.

Minutes seemed like hours. A man returned. "Rainer and Klaus are gone. They've taken several weapons."

"What could he be doing?" Judd said.

Westin pointed at the screen. "Watch."

Vicki waited for an answer from Tsion Ben-Judah as the others watched the latest news from GCNN. Because of the intense heat, many television transmissions had been interrupted. During the plague, the kids had usually seen coverage only at night. Now that the plague was over, it was clear the Global Community in the United North American States wanted to show they were back in control.

The sight of Kruno Fulcire turned Vicki's stomach. He had been the man responsible for her friend Pete's death, as well as hundreds of other believers who had fallen into the man's clutches. It was almost as if the military and political leaders around the world were having a contest to see who could kill believers faster.

Fulcire had chosen to be photographed near a small lake behind one of the many GC headquarters. A fountain sprayed water into the air, and Vicki couldn't help smirking as he beamed at the applause of the press corps.

"Looks like he's got water shooting out his head," Zeke said.

"Wouldn't hurt his brain any," Conrad said. "He probably doesn't have one."

"Let's keep it quiet," Marshall said.

Fulcire had no notes, charts, or graphs. He simply stood at the podium and smiled. "What a beautiful day." Laughter rippled through the crowd. "And every day is a great day to serve the risen lord Carpathia."

There were enough followers of Nicolae present to break into a hearty rendition of "Hail Carpathia," but Fulcire sang off-key.

When they finished, Fulcire grabbed the microphone and began pacing. "The end of

THE PERILS OF LOVE

this unnatural weather phenomenon comes at a most important time. We believe the United North American States can and will become the most loyal region in all the world. And to do that, we need the help of citizens who have already given so much."

"I think I know what he's leading up to." Janie smirked. "And it won't be good for believers."

Fulcire beamed, as if Carpathia were watching. "Since we can once again move around in daylight hours, we would like you to report any citizen who has not yet complied with receiving the mark of our lord and risen king. Anyone discovering an unmarked civilian will receive triple the reward previously offered."

"Great, the price for our heads just went up," Conrad said.

"Think of all the Nicks we could make if we turned everybody here in," Zeke said.

Mark stuck his head in the room and motioned for Vicki. "You have an answer to your message to Tsion."

Vicki hurried to the computer on the other side of the room and pulled up Tsion's e-mail. That the man would answer her personally excited Vicki.

Vicki,

Thank you for your question about what will happen in the coming kingdom. As we draw nearer to that time, now only a year away, many people have the same concerns, so you have spurred me to teach more about this here in Petra.

Let me quickly give you some thoughts. Jesus said that people would be "marrying and giving in marriage" during the Tribulation just as they did during the days before the Flood. See Matthew 24:37-39. But as you know, many who become believers after the Rapture will be martyred for the cause of Christ and will be resurrected after the Glorious Appearing. Many others will survive the Tribulation and be "the sheep" Jesus referred to in Matthew 25:31-40 who go into the kingdom to populate the Millennium, or thousand-year reign of Christ. These, of course, will raise their children and possibly help with the raising of other children who survive but are under the age of accountability when Christ returns.

The story of the rich man in hell and Lazarus who was a believer—see Luke 16:19-31—is quite clear. In the next life we will still recognize not only those we

*knew on earth, but as Lazarus, he recog-
nized Abraham who had lived hundreds
of years before him. Even those in torment recognized those in paradise. That
would indicate we all will recognize one
another in the next life. Remember, Paul
said, "For me to depart and be with Christ
is far better." So we will have an even
better relationship then than we do now.*

*I know you still have Judd on your mind,
and believe me, we are praying for you
both. Whether God allows you to marry or
not isn't the question. The question is, will
you trust him for your future? God can use
you in the kingdom after his second coming, or he can use you in heaven. Trust
him to be faithful.*

*Yours in Christ,
Tsion Ben-Judah*

As Kruno Fulcire finished his press conference, a wave of hope washed over Vicki like
a waterfall. Judd was in God's hands. Their
possible marriage was too. And all believers
from Wisconsin to the remote parts of the
world. No matter how much money the Global
Community offered or how creative the GC
could get trying to catch unmarked civilians,
the believers still had God's protection.

✳

Judd watched the screens carefully for any sign of Rainer and Klaus. He hoped they would come to their senses and turn around, but Judd gasped when a manhole cover moved in the middle of the street a block away. Weapons plopped on the ground, and Rainer and Klaus crawled onto the street.

Helga gritted her teeth. "What in the world are they doing?"

A man to Judd's left shook his head. "Rainer likes to say, 'Life is a temporary assignment.'"

"He's going to make it a lot more temporary if he doesn't get out of there quickly," Helga said.

Rainer and Klaus moved behind a burned-out car. Automatic weapons fire sounded, and the two were up and running. The GC squad, at least a dozen officers strong, rounded the corner. Rainer fired over their heads.

"He could have killed several of them," Judd said. "Why didn't he?"

"Maybe he's not trying to kill them," Westin said. "Maybe he's trying to get them away from us."

Helga quickly switched to another camera

showing that the area around the safe house was clear. She pointed to Judd and Westin and looked at the older man to her left. "Take them to number two."

"We're not leaving," Westin said. "We'll stay and fight with the rest of you."

She looked hard at him. "I'm not arguing. You're the only pilot here and this guy—" she pointed to Judd—"has a fiancée waiting. Go."

The older man led them to the secret exit, and they climbed into a large tunnel. The man stuck out his hand. "Gunther Carr."

They walked west, away from the house, through stagnant water. Gunfire erupted again above them, and GC officers' yells echoed in the cavern.

"What's number two?" Judd whispered.

"An underground bunker," Gunther said. "It's dark and stinks down there, but at least you'll be safe."

More gunfire. Judd prayed for Rainer and Klaus. He had no idea if he would ever see them again.

FOUR

Rainer's Sacrifice

JUDD and Westin spent the night alone in the underground chamber. They were anxious to know what had happened to their friends but didn't dare go into the tunnel. The maze of pipes leading from their area made it nearly impossible to go back without someone leading them.

"What happens if the GC find the house and everybody's killed?" Judd said.

Westin shrugged and paced the room like a nervous animal. Gunther had shown them where to find food and flashlights, but they felt trapped with no contact with the outside world. Judd's phone didn't work in the enclosed space, and there was no computer hookup. Westin found a small television stashed in a cabinet, but it didn't work.

"Great, we can't even hear the GC's lies," Westin said.

After spending the evening praying for their new friends, Judd tried to get some sleep. Finally he sat up. Westin was reading something by the fading glow of a flashlight. "What do you think about our chances of getting out of New Babylon alive?"

Westin yawned. "We improved our chances by coming in here, but I don't like the fact that we let those people fight for us."

"What are you reading?"

Westin held up a weathered New Testament and Psalms he had discovered. "I found this psalm about how God heals the broken-hearted, counts the stars, supports the humble, and feeds the animals. Then I came to this:

> "The strength of a horse does not impress
> him;
> how puny in his sight is the strength
> of a man.
> Rather, the Lord's delight is in those
> who honor him,
> those who put their hope in his unfailing
> love."

"That's good," Judd said.

Westin ran a hand through his hair. "You know, when I believed what you and Lionel told me, there was part of me that thought I was pretty hot stuff. Being a pilot for the rich and famous, able to get you guys access wherever I wanted . . . Even when I started working with the Tribulation Force, I sort of felt like I was doing God a favor."

Judd smiled. "I know what you mean."

"And then I read a passage like this. If I really want to make God happy, I'll just trust him and let him use me however he wants. If it means I'm flying supplies, that's great. If it means I'm holed up in this dark, stinky septic tank, that's okay."

Judd nodded. "The biggest hurdle is believing God is real. Then you have to believe he really loves you and died to forgive you. Once I got that through my head, it was a lot easier to trust him, though it's not always easy."

It was after midnight when Judd heard footsteps echo in the tunnel. The door opened and Gunther entered with the rest of the group. One by one they crowded inside, some collapsing on the floor. Rainer and Klaus weren't with them.

"We need to stay here for a while," Gunther said. "The Peacekeepers are back, but we're hoping they won't find our hideout."

"What about Rainer and Klaus?" Westin said.

"They're dead."

"But not before they took a half dozen GC with them," a younger man said.

"What happened?" Judd said.

"Rainer and Klaus tried to get the GC to chase them away from the safe house," Gunther said. "It worked for a while, but then the GC surrounded them. After a firefight, the GC won."

"We're kicking ourselves for not going to their rescue," Helga said. "We should have at least used the remote guns."

"You know that wouldn't have done any good," Gunther said.

Judd thought of Rainer's wife. They were together now, reunited in heaven.

"Why didn't you set off the booby traps?" Westin said.

Helga sat forward and took some beef jerky from a tin. "We left the entrance on automatic. If the GC find it and crawl inside, the whole place will go up. All the evidence will be destroyed."

※

Vicki waited for word from Judd and agonized when she didn't hear anything. She spent the entire night waiting by the computer, dialing Judd's number, but getting nothing.

As the sun rose the next morning, she lay in bed, thinking of Tsion's e-mail. Something he had said was running around in her head. Between that and news of Judd, she knew she wouldn't be able to sleep.

"Thinking about Judd?" Shelly whispered from the cot next to Vicki's.

"I'm thinking about a lot of stuff," Vicki said.

"It's good to see *you* tied up for a change. You always have your stuff together."

"If you only knew."

"So what is it?" Shelly said, sitting up.

"I'll tell you if you tell me what happened between you and Conrad. You guys were close, and then everything went south."

"I wouldn't want to jinx you and Judd," Shelly said.

"What do you mean?"

Shelly sighed. "Conrad's sweet. He's a little younger than me but really mature in a lot of ways. The closer we got and the more time we spent together, the more serious things became."

"He popped the question and you said no?"

"Not exactly." Shelly opened her mouth like she wanted to say something but looked at the floor. "This is really hard."

"Shel, what is it?"

She paused a moment more, then looked at Vicki. "We were fixing up one of the cabins with Charlie—this was before the heat wave and before Judd came back. Charlie ran for some supplies, and Conrad asked if he could kiss me. I got kind of uncomfortable. We had both said we wouldn't put ourselves in a situation where we were alone together, you know, so we wouldn't be tempted. When I hesitated, he thought I didn't like him anymore. Then I tried to explain and things really got bad. I know it was only a kiss, but I just didn't feel right."

"You guys talked after that, right?"

"Shouted is more like it. He said if I didn't trust him that we should break things off and just be friends. But we haven't been, and I don't see that changing anytime soon."

"Maybe if you brought Marshall or Becky in on it, they could help resolve it."

"I feel so hurt by the whole thing, and I know he's hurt too."

"I think you did the right thing saying no," Vicki said. "Something in your gut told you it didn't feel right."

"But Conrad's nice. He would never do anything—"

"Doesn't matter," Vicki said. "If you feel something's not good and you push that down, you stop listening to the voice God gave you."

"What do you mean, 'voice'?"

"I think God gives us something inside that tells us when things don't feel right. The times when I got into the most trouble, before I became a believer, were times when I didn't listen to that feeling, that voice that was telling me to watch out. And I know a lot of other girls who've had those same feelings but didn't listen to them because they were afraid they'd hurt somebody's feelings."

"So I wasn't crazy to say no?"

"I don't think so. And if Conrad loved you, he'd understand. Maybe he feels just as bad about it as you do. You won't know until you talk."

Shelly nodded and stared into the darkness. "Maybe I will." She turned to Vicki. "Now your turn."

Vicki waved a hand. "It's nothing compared to—"

"No fair, you promised."

Vicki rolled her eyes. "Well, the main thing is Judd. I don't understand why he hasn't called. If he's hurt or something I'll understand, but . . ."

"Judd wouldn't leave you hanging if he didn't have a good reason."

"You're right. But there's something else.

Tsion wrote back and told me what he thought would happen after the Glorious Appearing. I mean, if Judd and I do get married, will we still be married after Jesus comes back? Could we have children? There's all kinds of questions, and the return of Christ is only a year away."

Shelly bit her lip. "Does make you think, doesn't it?"

Vicki pulled out a copy of Tsion's e-mail she had printed and turned on her flashlight. "He's talking about people who will go into the Millennium alive—"

"What's the mill . . . milla . . . what you said?"

"A millennium is a thousand years. When Jesus comes back at the Glorious Appearing, he's going to reign a thousand years before the time of judgment."

"And the thousand years starts after the battle of Armageddon, right?"

"Exactly."

"So what did he say?"

"Listen to this. 'These, of course, will raise their children and possibly help with the raising of other children who survive but are under the age of accountability when he returns.'"

Shelly leaned forward. "I don't get it. What's the accountability thing?"

"Tsion believes there will be kids alive who

aren't believers but are too young to really understand the gospel."

"Okay."

"I had a dream once before we found the schoolhouse. I wanted to take in as many people as we could and teach them. Even unbelievers. We were able to take in quite a few—Melinda, Lenore, and the others—but I always felt drawn to kids."

"And you want to do that after Jesus comes back?"

Vicki frowned. "I don't know how it would happen or even where, but wouldn't it be exciting to take care of kids who don't have parents? Kids who were just like we were after the Rapture?"

Shelly raised her eyebrows. "You think you can get Judd to sign off on the idea?"

"It's probably just stupid—"

"Don't say that," Shelly said. "You've always said if God plants an idea in your head, no matter what other people think, he can help you accomplish it."

Vicki lay back on the bed. "I wish I could talk about it with Judd."

For two more days Judd and the others stayed holed up in the underground compartment because of GC activity above. Many in the group wept for Rainer and Klaus, blaming themselves for not going after them.

Judd thought of Chang. If he could get word to him about their trouble, Chang could do something. But Judd hadn't told anyone he knew a believer inside the palace, and he feared that he might endanger Chang by dragging him into their problem. Judd decided he would only bring up Chang as a last resort.

Judd recalled the envelope Rainer had given him, and he opened it while the others were asleep. Inside was another envelope and a note attached to it.

> Judd,
>
> I wrote this to Otto after we talked. Klaus and I are going to try to lure the GC away. Please give this letter to Otto if you can. And tell Vicki about me when you see her.
>
> In Christ,
> Rainer

After dark, on the third day, Judd followed the others through the sewers to the safe house. They had heard no explosions, so they figured the GC hadn't discovered the hideout.

One by one they crawled through the

secret opening and entered the house. Everyone tried to squeeze into the computer room, though some had to remain in the hall. The computers were off, and Helga guessed there had been a power outage.

She fired up the computer with the biggest monitor and clicked on the security cameras. "That's strange. I can't get any of them to work."

"Maybe the outage affected the cameras and they have to be reset," someone said.

Helga scratched her head. "Something seems different."

"Work on it and we'll get some food," Gunther said. "Depending on how long the power was off, some of it may be spoiled."

Helga tried to pull up the Global Community News Network, but it wouldn't work. "Judd, do me a favor and open the secret entrance, then close it and come right back."

Judd hurried and did what he was told.

When he returned, Helga had a strange look on her face. "You opened it all the way, right?"

"Yeah. What's wrong?"

"The alarm isn't working on the computer."

A group rushed down the hall, and Judd thought someone was coming with food.

Then he heard the click of rifles and shouts from the kitchen. Helga jumped up and darted for the hall but stopped dead in her tracks.

A GC Peacekeeper stuck a gun through the door. "On the floor! Now!"

FIVE

Captured

JUDD was stunned at the sight of uniformed Peacekeepers running through the hideout. He hit the floor and watched black boots surround him and Helga. An officer patted them down and took Judd's cell phone. "On your feet and up the stairs."

The moon shone brightly as Judd climbed out and joined the others. Several squad cars with their lights on were parked in front of the house, illuminating the line of prisoners. A Peacekeeper ordered them to sit, then pointed a flashlight at their foreheads and their right hands, checking for the mark of Carpathia.

Judd knew he should feel scared, but a sense of peace came over him. He almost felt relieved that the running and hiding were over.

He thought of Vicki and regretted risking this trip. He had been trying to call her since they had gone into hiding, but his phone didn't work underground. Now he would never again tell her he loved her. He wondered if the GC would make examples of them and show their executions on television. Or would the GC just get things over right here? The believers were outnumbered, and the GC had so many weapons.

A man with several military medals pinned to his uniform stepped forward, hands clasped behind his back. "I suppose you're wondering why your little operation didn't explode when we entered, hmm?"

When no one answered, the man gave a fake smile and continued. "Well, I'll tell you. After your two friends gave us trouble, we found your guns." He motioned overhead. "When we uncovered your entrance, instead of barging in, we called in the bomb squad." He pointed to the side of the house, and Judd saw a gaping hole. "We made a new entrance—hope you don't mind—found your little bomb, defused it, and waited. What a shock when we heard you enter through the sewers."

Judd wondered if anyone would stand up to the officer, and he didn't have to wait long. Westin shook his head, and the man in charge kicked Westin hard. "Wipe that silly grin off your face!"

"You're going to lose," Westin said.

The officer squinted. "You have no guns, you have no contact with other rebels, and you have no chance of escape." He held up a small computer device. "And in this tiny drive I have all the information from your computers. Your contacts, your plans. Everything."

Helga gave the man a worried look. "Our files are encrypted. You'll never be able to—"

"With the resources of the Global Community? I'm sure our tech crew will have this figured out by my morning coffee." He turned to Westin. "You're crazy to think you can defeat us."

"You can kill us, but you're not going to win," Westin said.

"Ah, a Judah-ite, eh?" The man turned and spoke to the men holding guns on the group. "Followers of Tsion Ben-Judah. They believe in the God of the Bible and that he is punishing us for our sins. That sums it up, doesn't it, Judah-ite?"

"I believe one day every knee will bow and every tongue will confess that Jesus Christ is Lord."

"Amen," a few people whispered.

"Jesus Christ?" The officer tapped his lips with his index finger and looked at the other Peacekeepers. "Haven't seen him, have you?"

The others laughed.

"But I have seen someone come back from the dead. With my own eyes—not some fairy tale written thousands of years ago."

"One day you will kneel and admit that Jesus—"

The man punched Westin in the face. Westin slumped over and Judd reached out to help him, but the officer pushed Judd away with his boot. "Cuff them! Anybody so much as breathes, shoot them."

Peacekeepers moved behind the group and put plastic zip cuffs on each prisoner. Judd wondered if anyone would put up a fight or try to escape, but everyone seemed to submit to the procedure.

The lead officer spoke by radio to someone at headquarters. After a head count, he relayed how many they were bringing in and that GCNN cameras should be waiting for them.

"You think your superiors will be proud of the fact that we were living right here under your noses?" Westin said.

The man glared at Westin. "I promise you, today I will dance in your blood."

The group had all been cuffed except for

Judd and Gunther when the lights went out. Literally. Peacekeepers dropped their weapons and reached to rub their eyes as headlights on the GC cars went dark. Flashlights were useless to the officers. Streetlights disappeared. Judd had seen power outages before. Once his parents had been away and the power went out while he was watching a scary movie in the basement. It had taken him several minutes to find his way upstairs, and it had terrified him.

But this was different. Lights on phones, radios, the dashboards of the squad cars—everything was dark. The incredible thing was, Judd could still see. Everything was a hazy brown, and he could only see about twenty feet, but he could see.

This must be what a cat sees in the dark, Judd thought.

Some of the Peacekeepers still had their guns pointed toward the prisoners, but Judd could tell they were disoriented. One tapped his watch and punched a button, trying to see the time, but even the lighted display on his watch had gone dark.

"This is really weird," Westin whispered to Judd. "Can you see?"

"I can, but I don't think they can."

"What's going on?" a frantic Peacekeeper called out.

"Everybody hold your position and keep the prisoners where they are," the leader said.

"Did the lights go out or is it just me?" another Peacekeeper whispered.

If the situation weren't so serious, Judd would have laughed. As soon as the leader mentioned the prisoners, the Peacekeepers aimed their guns at where they thought Judd and the others were standing. It was like a military version of pin-the-tail-on-the-donkey, with men pointing guns in every direction.

The leader pulled out his cell phone but couldn't see the keypad. He reached for his radio microphone three times before he grabbed the cord and worked his way to the mike. "We have a situation here, Base, an electrical blackout."

A few seconds pause, then the dispatcher's stressed voice came on. It was clear things were just as bad at headquarters as they were here. "We have power here, but no visual—" Judd couldn't make out the rest because people at headquarters were screaming in the background.

Gunther lifted a hand and motioned the prisoners to the right. As one they crept past the puzzled Peacekeepers. Judd stopped a few feet away from a Peacekeeper and spotted a pair of pliers on the man's belt. He inched closer and grasped the tool, slowly lifting it from the man's belt. As Judd grabbed, the Peacekeeper whirled around and fired. The shot went over Judd's head and ricocheted off the burned-out safe house.

Judd jammed the pliers in his pocket, hit the ground, and put his hands over his ears. Other Peacekeepers opened fire on where they thought the prisoners were standing, but they either fired into the safe house or actually shot each other. Judd counted three Peacekeepers on the ground, writhing in pain.

"Hold your fire!" the leader said, pulling out his pistol and gingerly stepping forward. He felt the ground with each step, as if he were going to plunge off a cliff. "Prisoners, stay where you are!"

Judd rolled his eyes and tried to still his breathing. The leader was only a few feet away and inching toward Judd like a blind man.

Judd glanced at the sky. The moon had been out earlier, but now it was as if God had pulled down a shade on the heavens. Judd wondered what would happen the next morning when the sun came up. Would everyone in the world experience this?

Someone on the edge of the line screamed,

dropped his weapon, and clawed at his eyes. "I can't see anything! Somebody do something!"

Judd used the noise to quietly sneak away, backing down the hill toward the GC squad cars. He put his hand through an open window and pressed the horn, which sent the Peacekeepers jumping. Judd leaped behind the cruiser as a volley of gunfire came his way, flattening a tire and crashing through a windshield.

Gunther motioned Judd over, and Judd crawled to the group and pulled out the pliers.

"Let's get out of here," someone said.

"We have to get that computer drive from the leader before we go," Helga said.

Judd snipped the plastic cuffs from Westin's hands. "I saw where the guy put it," Judd said. "I'll go."

"I'll go with you," Westin said.

When Judd and Westin returned, the Peacekeepers were in even worse shape. Some were on their hands and knees, trying to find their way back to their cars.

Within a few minutes these arrogant, cocky men were like frightened schoolchildren. They flicked flashlights, fumbled for lighters, and held their hands as close to their faces as they could, all in a vain attempt to see. But nothing helped.

Judd recalled the verses about Jesus being the light of the world and felt pity for these foolish people who had chosen Nicolae over the true God. If there had been a fire in front of these people, they would have walked right through it, so great was their darkness.

Westin pointed to the lead officer, and Judd angled toward the man who sat mumbling on a smoldering piece of wood. He had put his pistol back in its holster and was staring into the darkness.

Westin grabbed the gun and Judd expected the man to lunge or shout, but he just kept mumbling. "My wife. She doesn't know where I am. We should get word to the others not to come out, not to go into the dark."

Judd took out his pocketknife and carefully cut a hole in the man's right front pocket. The computer drive fell out. The Peacekeeper reached for his holster, but the gun was gone.

"You looking for this?" Westin whispered, cocking the gun close to the man's face. "Not dancing in any blood now, are you?"

"Please," the man cried, "don't take my gun."

Judd picked up the computer drive and

took a few steps back. Westin joined him, emptying the gun and tossing it back at the feet of the Peacekeeper. The man picked it up, pointed it at his own head, and pulled the trigger. He pulled again and again, until the clicking of the gun mocked him. The man broke down, falling to the ground and jerking with sobs.

"These people sure are scared of the dark, aren't they?" Westin said.

"It's not just the dark," Judd said. "They're separated from everybody else. It's like God has put them in their own little world."

Judd and Westin rejoined the group, and Gunther handed Judd his cell phone. They had decided to reenter the safe house and get as many supplies as they could.

Judd helped move food and water into the second hideout through the sewer. He was surprised to find he could see belowground just as he could above.

Helga destroyed the computers and cameras, saving one laptop for use in their next location. Gunther said they had a couple of options of where to go if the plague of darkness continued.

In moving and sifting through supplies, Judd found a Bible and stuffed it in his back pocket. He had studied Revelation intensely and vaguely remembered something about darkness but couldn't remember the reference.

He climbed upstairs for one last look before they headed for the sewer. Gunther and a few others had rigged up some explosives to destroy the safe house.

Judd pulled out his cell phone and dialed Vicki. When she answered on the first ring, he could tell by the emotion in her voice that she had been crying.

"I can't tell you everything right now, but I'm all right," Judd said. "Everything's going to be all right."

"What's that noise in the background?" Vicki said.

Judd looked at the Peacekeepers, many of whom were on the ground, screaming and cursing God. They scratched at unseen sores and rubbed their aching bodies. The pain that began as an itch soon turned so intense that the Peacekeepers crawled beside rocks or cars and tried to rub up against them for relief. Men chewed their tongues until blood ran down their chins. Some found rifles on the ground and turned them on themselves, hoping to end their agony.

"It's awful here, Vick," Judd said. He explained briefly what had happened. "Is it happening there too?"

"No, this is just supposed to occur in New Babylon."

"How do you know that?"

Judd heard a click of computer keys. "Here it is. It's in Revelation, chapter 16." Vicki read the verses, her voice trembling. " 'Then the fifth angel poured out his bowl on the throne of the beast, and his kingdom was plunged into darkness. And his subjects ground their teeth in anguish, and they cursed the God of heaven for their pains and sores. But they refused to repent of all their evil deeds.' "

"That's exactly what's happening," Judd said.

"Then get out of there," Vicki said, "and go back to Petra as fast as you can."

SIX

Judd's New Mission

JUDD and Westin jumped into the back of a squad car as Gunther and another member of the group got in the front. The rest of the group used the other vehicles.

Gunther had to drive slowly because he couldn't see very far. "Either of you know how long this is supposed to last?" Gunther said, looking in the rearview mirror.

Judd shook his head. "A friend of mine just read me the prophecy. From the stuff it says about people suffering, it sounds to me like it could be a while."

Gunther nodded. "That's what I think. Rainer and I talked about this. We both agreed when it happened, the end wasn't far away."

"What do you mean, 'the end'?" Westin said.

Gunther explained the prophecy about believers coming out of New Babylon. "The Lord predicts death and mourning and famine. Then it says he will destroy the city with fire. Rainer and I always thought that would be nuclear."

"If God's dropping his heavy artillery, we should get out," Westin said. "Maybe we could find a plane—"

Gunther held up a hand. "If Judd's right—and I think he is—we still have time to do some good here."

"What do you have in mind?" Judd said.

"Radios and computers are working," Gunther said. "We might be able to communicate with other locations and get the GC to release prisoners, maybe foul up their system. Plus, there's a holding facility not far from here. Captured Jews are sent to concentration camps from there. Since the heat wave ended, they've probably brought new people there."

"How do we know when to leave?" Judd said.

"The Lord will warn us. It's part of the prophecy. I know you two want to get back to Petra, but we could use the help."

Westin looked at Judd and shrugged. "If we can do some damage, I'm all for it."

Judd glanced at Gunther. "I need to make a phone call."

Vicki told the others about her conversation with Judd, and no sooner had they begun their prayer meeting for him than the phone rang. It was Judd again.

"Where are you?" Vicki said. "Tell me you've already gotten out of there."

"We're heading for another safe house, or at least where we think one is. It's pretty slow going."

"But you said—"

"Vick, Westin's plane was destroyed. I assume most of the GC planes were burned in the heat wave, though they probably have some stored somewhere. There's no way we're flying out of here today. The thing is—"

Vicki put a hand to her chest, feeling her heart suddenly drop. "Judd, you're not thinking of staying, are you?"

"Just hear me out." Judd explained what he knew about Gunther's plan. "There's a chance we might meet some unbelievers, those who haven't taken the mark yet."

"How?"

Judd explained the information about the holding facility. In the past few months, Vicki had heard more and more reports about rebels around the world, mostly Jews, who were transported to concentration camps rather than being put to death. The Global Community wanted to make them suffer for not taking Carpathia's mark and for simply being part of God's chosen people. The camps gave prisoners just enough food to keep them alive and tortured them daily. Vicki and Judd had talked about wanting to help these people, but she didn't think they would ever have the opportunity. But Vicki's first concern was Judd and getting him safely to Petra.

"What happens if the lights come back on?" Vicki said. "The GC will kill you and anyone else with you."

"I don't know if this is what I should do or not, but . . ." Judd's voice trailed off, and Vicki heard brakes squeal. Then someone said something, and car doors opened and closed.

"What's happening?" Vicki said.

"We're at one of the mark application centers," Judd said. "The others are going to see if they can destroy some equipment. It's not much, but every little bit helps."

Vicki closed her eyes tightly. "Judd, if God's leading you into this, you know I wouldn't want to stop you, but I'm scared."

"Believe me, the last thing I want to do is risk being separated from you. I found the perfect spot in Petra. You should see it. It's just that . . ." Judd's voice trailed off again.

When he could talk, he said, "I keep thinking about somebody out there crying out to God, behind bars or wherever, asking God for help, pleading with him to send someone. Maybe there's nobody there, but while this place is dark, I feel like I need to try."

Everything inside Vicki screamed for Judd to get to safety, but she knew if she were in the same position, she would want Judd's support. Finally, she said, "Go. Set as many captives free as you can. That's what we're supposed to be doing anyway, right?"

"Vick, I love you."

***

When Judd hung up, Gunther and the others were returning to the car.

Westin hopped in with a smile and slammed the door. "They won't be doing any marking of citizens in that place for a long time."

"Were there any people in there?" Judd said.

"Lots of them on the ground, screaming. Must have scared them half to death when we came waltzing in and smashed their equipment and took that head chopper apart." Westin looked at Judd. "You square things up with the little woman?"

Judd smiled. "She told me to go for it. When do we head that way?"

"Right now," Gunther said. He radioed the others, speaking in code, and told them where they were going.

"Why don't we just go to the palace?" Judd said.

Gunther shook his head. "We have no idea what kind of power Carpathia might have over this plague. Let's stick to trying to wreak havoc out here and maybe set a few people free."

The drive took longer than any of them expected. After three hours of navigating the streets at a slow speed, Gunther stopped outside a restaurant. "Nicolae himself is said to have eaten here with a few of his advisors. Come on."

Judd stepped out of the car and felt his flesh crawl. He had been to haunted houses as a kid and had heard the screams of frightened trick-or-treaters around Halloween, but he had never heard anything this eerie. People in torment had collapsed on the sidewalk. Some called from inside houses or businesses, pleading for help.

"Oh, Nicolae, you have all power," an older woman cried from across the street. "You bring light and peace and hope. Please, Nicolae, save us!"

"Shut up, woman!" a young man said. He was sitting with his back against the wall of a building next to the restaurant. "Neither Nicolae nor Fortunato can save you from this."

"Blasphemer!" an older man yelled. "You let Nicolae or any of his Peacekeepers hear you say that and you're a dead man."

The young man scratched at a bloody scab on his neck. "Death would be welcomed right now."

"I'm so hungry!" the old woman shouted. "Can someone bring me something?"

"Come on," Gunther said. "Don't pay attention to them."

"Who is that?" the young man said. "How can you drive a car when you can't even see?"

Gunther and the others went inside the restaurant, stepping over two bodies of people who had killed themselves. Judd stayed behind and inspected the young man's forehead. No mark. But when Judd leaned down and caught a glimpse of the man's right hand, he saw the clear mark of Carpathia.

The young man took a swipe at the air, missing Judd's head by inches. "Who are you? What do you want?" He had pulled his shirt up and was rubbing up against the coarse brick, trying to get some relief. His back was bleeding.

"I'm a friend," Judd said softly. "You don't have to be afraid."

"Do you have a gun?"

"No."

"Can you get one?"

"What for?"

The young man laughed wildly. "How long has it been since this darkness came? A week? Two?"

"It's only been a few hours," Judd said.

The man put a finger in his mouth and bit down hard. Blood poured from the wound and gushed down his lips. "I can't see to take a step, and I don't have the energy if I could. I just want to die. I know this is the end."

Judd stood and took a step toward the restaurant door.

"Please, I beg you. Hit me with something, knock me out. I can't stand this itching, and my head feels like it's about to burst!"

"I can't help you," Judd said. "I wish you'd have responded to God before it was too—"

"God?" the man screamed. "Jesus? I hate them! I hate everyone who talks about God!"

Judd walked away as the man cursed God, chewed his tongue, and smacked his head against the brick wall. Judd stepped over bodies and went inside the restaurant. Some people had been inside when the plague of darkness hit, and they were still moaning and wailing on the floor, under tables, and lying on booths.

Judd found Gunther and the others in the kitchen, cooking meat on the grill. The cook lay in the back, not moving. Some people had crawled inside the back door searching for food. One man near the grill had burned both his hands, not seeing the fire.

While Gunther cooked the meat, Judd and Westin gathered bread and drinks and headed for the car. Judd looked for the young man by the wall, but he had moved away.

When they were all inside the car, Judd tore off a piece of French bread and grabbed one of the still-sizzling pieces of meat from Gunther. The smell of the food made Judd's mouth water.

Gunther put the car in gear, and they rolled over something. At first Judd thought they had been too close to the curb, but when he looked through the back window, he saw the young man lying on the street. He had crawled under the tires and now lay life-less on the road.

Everywhere they drove, Judd heard howls from people in pain. It seemed to be getting worse by the hour. When people heard the car's engine, they ran into the street, reaching out like blind zombies, trying anything to relieve their pain. Judd hated ignoring them, but what could they do? These people had chosen against God and were now paying the price.

Judd wondered what it was about the darkness that made things so much worse. Simply turning out the lights on the world was one thing, but there was something supernatural about this that caused people enough pain to want to kill themselves.

The car stopped a half hour later in front of a guard hut. Judd couldn't see the building inside, but security fences with razor wire on top ran as far as he could see.

"I can't guarantee your safety in there," Gunther said.

"No way I'm missing this," Westin said.

"Me either," Judd said.

"Then let's go."

Gunther pulled up to the gate and opened his door. Someone inside the guard shack yelled, "Halt! Who goes there?"

Gunther didn't respond but went into a crouch and stuck his head into the doorway.

"Identify yourself or I'll shoot!" the guard said.

Gunther waved at Westin, and the pilot got

out and went to the front of the car. "Why would you want to shoot—?"

Blam!

The gun's explosion sent Westin to the ground. The guard hobbled out of the shack like a drunken man, waving the gun and threatening to shoot again. With a swift movement, Gunther jumped, kicked, and the gun clattered on concrete.

The guard screamed in pain and fell in a heap. "Who are you? What do you want here?"

Judd got out as Gunther stepped toward the guard and said, "Where are the rebels you're holding?"

The guard's eyes widened. "I don't know what you're talking about."

"Right," Gunther said, picking up the gun. He walked into the shack and flipped a lever, opening the gate.

"You can see?" the guard said.

"Do you want me to shoot you?" Gunther said.

A wide grin spread across the man's face. "Yes. I'd like that. Please go ahead."

Gunther frowned and looked at Judd. "Help me tie him up. We'll find them ourselves."

SEVEN

Zvi

JUDD followed the others through the fence and toward a huge building. The stone structure had survived the heat wave, and by the numbers of burned-out cars nearby, Judd guessed some had survived the heat by running inside.

They met two guards at the front entrance who were writhing on the floor, scratching their bodies, and moaning in pain. Instead of tying or cuffing them, Gunther and Westin retrieved their guns and proceeded down the hall.

"How are we ever going to find where they're holding the prisoners?" Westin said.

Gunther placed a finger to his lips and pointed at a female guard with her head on a desk at the end of the hall. As they approached, the woman sat up and looked wildly in their direction. "Who's there?"

"It's all right, Sergeant. Don't be afraid."

"How can you see me?"

Gunther ignored the question. "We come on a mission from the potentate. There have been several rebels arrested in the past few days. They are awaiting transport?"

The woman grimaced and grabbed the back of her neck in pain. "Most of them were taken yesterday. There are seven left in the holding cell downstairs."

"I would like to see them."

"You have to have authorization. I don't even know who you are."

"Believe me, this request comes from the highest levels—from the potentate himself." Paper rattled and Gunther handed the sergeant something.

"I can't see this," she said. "How do I know you're telling the truth?"

"I could have disarmed you the moment I came in. You must trust me. Now if you will point me in the right direction—"

"I don't know which direction the stairs are. I'm all turned around."

"Hand me your key card and I'll let myself in."

"I'm not supposed to give that to anyone," she said.

"We both agree—these are extraordinary circumstances," Gunther said. "I'll be back."

The woman hesitated, then took off her plastic card and held it out.

Gunther motioned Judd and the others toward the stairwell, and they crept along as quietly as possible.

"What are you going to do to those prisoners?" she said. "They're just Jews."

"I want to talk with them. To see if I can't persuade them to come over to our way of thinking."

As Judd reached the door, the woman tilted her head and scratched her neck. "If you ask me, we should just kill them now and get it over. They're going to die one way or another."

"Yes, thank you for that advice."

"Wait. Does the potentate know when this darkness will stop?"

"We don't know when things will return to normal, but you can be sure the potentate only has your best interests at heart." Gunther walked toward the door and inserted the card.

Going down the stairs was like walking through a dense cloud. After going through several doors and walking down a narrow hallway, Judd pointed to his right, toward a series of cells. At the end was a large cell Judd thought would hold at least a hundred prisoners. Only seven men lay on cots or on the floor. Judd looked for the mark of the believer but saw none. But only three of the men had the mark of Carpathia.

"When will you turn on the lights?" a man yelled. "This is cruel and unusual."

The others in the cell shouted at the man to be quiet.

Gunther spoke calmly and without emotion. "Gentlemen, we are not with the Global Community. We represent the true potentate of the universe."

"Were you the ones who turned out the lights?" a younger man said.

"No. In fact we were about to be arrested by Peacekeepers when this plague of darkness began. God has enabled us to see, while those without his protection cannot."

"I am a religious man," another said. "Why would God give you special treatment?"

Another man grabbed the cell bars and pulled himself up. He had scratch marks about his face and neck. "Stop all this talking and let us out. You know what the GC will do to us if we're kept here."

Gunther asked Westin to find out how to release the cell door, then pulled a chair close to the cell. The men inside grew impatient. One with long hair stayed back, wary of Gunther's voice.

"How do we know you're not the GC with more of your tricks?" Longhair said.

"We come in the name of the Prince of Peace, the King of kings, the one who was called the Light of the World."

"Who is this light?" a bearded man said. "And when can he come down here?"

Gunther chuckled. "I will tell you about this light. In the beginning the Word already existed. He was with God, and he was God. He was in the beginning with God. He created everything there is. Nothing exists that he didn't make. Life itself was in him, and this life gives light to everyone. The light shines through the darkness, and the darkness can never extinguish it."

"Don't talk to us of light and life when we are locked away in darkness so thick you can taste it," a man said.

Others shushed him and asked Gunther to continue.

"We come on behalf of this light to ask you to gain true freedom, true sight. There is a reason why we can see—"

"You can't see any more than we can."

"Then how can I tell you're wearing a pendant around your neck? And that your hair is down to your shoulders—and you're closing your eyes—no, opening."

"None of us can see. Do you have special glasses or something?"

The man at the back stood. "Let us out of here and we'll listen to you."

"Soon," Gunther said. "But first let me tell you that the one who sent us made the world, but when he came, the world didn't recognize him. Even in his own land and among his own people, he was not accepted. But to all who believed him and accepted him, he gave the right to become children of God. They are reborn! This is not a physical birth—this rebirth comes from God."

"I've heard these words before from that traitor Tsion Ben-Judah," the bearded man said. "It was his fault the Global Community came after us in the first place."

The cell door began to move, and the men jumped to their feet. Westin came back as the men groped toward the opening, falling over cots and each other.

"We can show you the true light," Gunther said while the men poured out of the cell. "If you don't receive this gift God is offering, you are destined to live in darkness forever."

"I'll take my chances," the bearded man said.

The three with the mark of Carpathia left immediately. The four others held out their hands, searching for a wall or anything that could guide them.

A young man stopped near Gunther and Judd. "You say there's a way for us to see, even in this blackness?"

Judd touched Gunther's arm. "Can I talk to him?"

Gunther smiled and nodded.

"My name's Judd. Put out your hand." The man did and Judd shook it. "I'll lead you out of here. We'll talk outside."

As they went through the hallways and up the stairs, Judd learned the man's name was Zvi Zeidman.

"When the mark of Carpathia came, I went underground with some friends," Zvi said. "We could sense hostility toward Israelis. When the heat wave hit, others joined us, but someone gave us up for the reward."

Judd paused at the top of the stairs and noticed the female guard was not at her post. They walked to the front of the building and heard gunfire. The few guards left were hunkered down, firing at any noise.

"It'll be best to stay here until they run out of ammunition," Judd said. He found an open office and sat Zvi on a cushioned chair.

"I don't know why I feel better having someone who can see," Zvi said. "In the cell

I had started to itch and get a tremendous headache."

Judd got the man some water and sat behind the desk. Though Zvi was in his twenties, he looked much older and had dark, curly hair and deep-set eyes.

Zvi put his head back. "How can you see?"

"I don't see fully," Judd said. "Everything's kind of brown. But I can see this computer screen and . . ." Judd studied the screen closely. He clicked on an e-mail message and pulled it up.

"What is it?" Zvi said.

"This office must belong to one of the prison directors."

About halfway into the message Judd spotted an interesting paragraph.

> Regarding the latest Jewish camp on the Island, I wish to relate good news. The transport you sent arrived fine with only two dead prisoners. We have experienced great success in keeping the inmates alive and, at the same time, miserable. The camp doctor has come up with a concoction that we have to feed only once a day, and it sustains the prisoners for twenty-four hours.

Judd read on, discovering this mysterious "Island" had more than two thousand housed there. A chill ran down his back. He wondered if the camp was under the plague of darkness, and if so, what people were doing.

"What are you reading?" Zvi said.

"Have you heard of the Island?"

"Yes. It's on the Tigris. I have heard horror stories of Jews being taken there. I'm not sure which is worse, being taken to the Island or facing the guillotine. At least with the blade, the suffering is over."

"What else have you heard about the camps?" Judd said.

Zvi put his hands behind his head and leaned back. "It's worse than the Nazis in the 1930s and 1940s. The GC torture their prisoners to the point of death but don't allow them the decency of dying. I've even heard they take videos of the beatings and torture and send them to Carpathia."

Judd shook his head. He wished he could do something for people on the Island, but he decided he had to focus on Zvi. Random gunfire echoed through the hallway, and Judd moved closer. "You don't have to stay in the dark. God can open your eyes."

"You going to preach now? Like that guy did back in the cell?"

"We've risked our lives to come here

because we thought there might still be someone who needed to accept God's forgiveness."

Zvi rolled his eyes and bit his lip, then seemed to remember that Judd could see his face. He put his head in his hands.

Judd paused, then continued. "Before I found out about God, I used to hate it when people would preach or act like they knew something I didn't. I don't want to come across that way. There was a time when I felt really nervous about talking about God, and I tried to figure out all kinds of ways to convince people without making them feel bad."

"And what do you do now?"

"The world's gone so crazy that there's no time to tiptoe. I just lay it out before people as plainly as I can and let them make their decision."

"Okay, so lay it out."

"Basically, God loves you and wants you to be his child. He wants to adopt you into his family, but he won't do that unless you want to be a part of it."

"What do you mean?"

"God's perfect. He can't allow anything near him that's imperfect. And you and I are both sinful. We've done bad things."

"I've been taught since I was young that

the path to God was through obeying his commands."

"True, but you know as well as I do that you haven't lived up to every command. And if you break even one, you're out of the program. That's why God had to provide a sacrifice, so we could be forgiven."

"This is the part where you tell me about Jesus, how he is the Messiah, and if I'll just get baptized or pray some prayer—"

"Zvi, have you ever considered the possibility that you've been living in darkness your whole life? Do you know God's peace, feel his forgiveness, his love?"

"You can't know those things in this life."

"Yes, you can. Again, I'm not trying to preach, and this is your decision, but God is real and he wants to come into your life right now and make a difference. He wants to show you mercy, but you have to accept it. I've met a lot of people in the past few years who've been raised exactly like you, and when they see the truth, they can't believe they were blind to it for so long."

Zvi sighed. "And you guarantee relief from the darkness?"

Judd smiled. "It's one of the perks. Back when the stinging locusts came—" Judd stopped as someone approached in the hall.

"I heard you talking," a woman said. A gun clicked. "Tell me where you are! Come out now or I'll shoot!"

EIGHT

The Blind See

JUDD sat still as the female guard stumbled down the hall, her gun held in the air, the other hand out to guide her. Judd leaned close to Zvi and whispered, "Don't make a sound." But when Judd leaned back, the chair squeaked.

The woman pointed the gun at him. "I heard that! Come out of the director's office, hands up!"

Judd studied the angle of the gun. She was aiming about three feet over their heads. He thought of rushing the woman or hiding behind the desk, but neither of the options seemed good.

Judd turned and picked up a beautiful glass paperweight from the desk. The delicate piece was about the size of a baseball and had been created in the likeness of Nicolae

Carpathia. Judd carefully brought the object behind his head and threw it over the woman's head. It crashed against the wall, shattering into a million pieces.

The woman screamed and turned, firing at the wall. The bullet pinged through the hallway. Judd jumped up, lunged for the door, and slammed it. He turned the lock and dived for the ground as another bullet punctured the wall above his head. Judd hit the floor and pulled Zvi down with him.

Zvi was panicking now, breathing heavily and shaking. "A friend told me he saw a man appear at one of the mass beheadings of Judah-ites. Right out of thin air. He wasn't there, and then he was. Do you think that was from God?"

"What did the man say?"

"He talked about God's forgiveness, like you."

"I've seen angels do the same thing," Judd said. "They come as God's messengers to warn people about not taking Carpathia's mark. And they plead with the undecided to choose Christ. It's another display of God's love."

"I won't take Carpathia's mark."

"It's not enough to be against Nicolae. Jesus said those who are not for him are against him. That puts you in some pretty awful company."

Judd could tell by the look on Zvi's face that there was a fierce battle raging. He had seen the same look many times before. Those who rejected Christ seldom struggled like this. They simply threw their hands in the air and walked away. But Zvi was different.

The woman outside cried and moaned. The gun clicked over and over. Judd opened the door to find her lying on the floor, her face buried in her arms. She had pointed the gun at her head and was pulling the trigger.

"I'll be right back," Judd whispered to Zvi.

Judd crawled on the tile floor, scooting on his knees and pulling himself forward with his hands.

The woman looked wild, clawing at her skin until it bled. Big patches of hair were gone from her head. "Oh, God, help me. I don't want to go through another one of these!" She finally stopped and put out a hand toward Judd. "Who are you?"

"A friend. Don't be afraid. I'm not going to hurt you."

"You're one of them, aren't you? One of the Judah-ites."

Judd didn't answer. He simply stared at the

-6 on her forehead, signifying that she was from the United North American States.

"Before the disappearances, before any of the bad things started happening, I went to one of those big meetings," she said. "The kind they used to have in stadiums." Saliva ran down the woman's lips and onto her chin. She was sobbing as she talked, reaching out, then pulling her hand back.

"A man sang and then another one stood up and talked about the Bible. I didn't want any part of it. My friends and I were there to make fun of the meeting. And then I saw some people from my neighborhood going forward. I almost went with them, just to see what would happen. I almost did."

"Why didn't you?" Judd said.

"I thought religion was for weak people. I thought I had plenty of time to decide. I wanted to have fun with my life. But . . ."

With this, the woman flew into a frenzy of scratching and wailing. Her eyes flew open and Judd saw how hollow they looked, as if he could see all the way to her soul.

When she settled, Judd came closer. "Let me help you to a safe place."

"Where can I go in this blackness that's safe?" she spat. "I might as well throw myself off the side of the building. There's no hope!"

Judd wanted to tell her she could call out to God and be forgiven, but he couldn't. The best he could do for her was ease her pain a little.

"I know what I've done!" the woman yelled. "I had a lot of chances to say yes to God, but I kept putting it off. Kept saying no. And now look what happened."

Judd sat back, drained of emotion. How many other people on earth could say the same thing? How many had hardened their hearts toward God, making jokes of the message or saying they would get around to it later? Judd had been one of them. He had ignored the truth for so long, but God had given him a second chance.

Judd scampered back to the office and helped Zvi to his feet. "Come on. We have to help this lady."

Judd pulled him into the hall, and they both helped the guard to her feet. Judd found a lunchroom down the hall and put the woman in a chair. "There's a refrigerator behind you, to your right. Looked like there were some sandwiches in there. And here's a drink in case you're thirsty."

The woman reached out and nearly knocked the can of soda over. She took a sip, sat back, and mumbled something.

"What did you say?"

"I know he tried to reach me," the woman whispered. "I watched them bring people through here and treat them like dogs, then talk about peace and love and goodwill. I knew in my heart it was fake and the other message was true." She looked up and opened her mouth. Her chin quivered as she tried to form the words. Then tears welled in her eyes.

Judd guessed what she was trying to say. She wanted to know if there was any hope, if God would somehow give her one more chance. But the woman must have known the answer. She put her head on the table and sobbed.

Judd put an arm around Zvi and guided him to the door. As they walked down the long hall, the woman's wails and cries nearly tore Judd's heart out.

When they reached the police cruiser and the others, Judd found Gunther and explained what he had seen on the computer in the director's office. Gunther and Westin went back inside to investigate while Judd and Zvi climbed into the GC cruiser.

"How could you have compassion for that woman when she wanted to kill you?" Zvi said.

"Because I was exactly like her before the

disappearances. For some reason, God gave me mercy and allowed me to call on him before it was too late."

"Why do I still have a chance when that woman doesn't?"

"I don't know the full answer, but I do know that if God has given you one more opportunity to respond, do it."

Zvi turned his head toward the window, deep in thought. "Tell me why you think Jesus is the Messiah."

Judd began in the Old Testament and from memory shared many prophecies that looked forward to the Messiah. "In Genesis, God curses the serpent and says that a descendent of Eve will crush the serpent's head. Jesus won the victory over the devil on the cross. In Isaiah it's predicted that a virgin will conceive a child and give birth to a son. Mary, Jesus' mother, was a virgin.

"In one of the little books, Micah, I think, it says that out of Bethlehem will come a ruler over Israel whose origins are from ancient times. Jesus was born in Bethlehem."

"But wasn't Jesus just a good teacher? He never really claimed to be the Messiah, did he?"

"That was the reason the Jewish leaders were so angry. He called God his Father. He said, 'I existed before Abraham was even born,' which is how God referred to himself to Moses. It drove them wild. They wanted to kill him."

"But did Jesus actually say he was the Messiah?"

"In one of the Gospels, John the Baptist sent someone to ask that very question. It was something like, 'John wants to know if you're the one who was to come, or if we should expect somebody else.' "

"What did Jesus say?"

"I'm going from memory here, but it was something like, 'Go back and tell John that the blind can see, the lame can walk, the deaf hear, and the good news—' "

" '—is preached to the poor,' " Zvi finished. "I know that passage. Isaiah 61." He closed his eyes. " 'The Spirit of the Sovereign Lord is upon me, because the Lord has appointed me to bring good news to the poor. He has sent me to comfort the broken-hearted and to announce that captives will be released and prisoners will be freed. . . .' "

"It's exactly what he's done for you today, Zvi. God has freed you from your prison so you can respond to him. So you can know him. So you can be forgiven."

Zvi stared into the darkness. "Give me a moment."

Judd nodded. "I'll be right back."

Judd stepped out of the car and said a prayer for Zvi, then dialed Chang Wong's secure phone and reached him at his apartment.

"Judd, your worries are over," Chang said. "I've finally decided it's time for me to get out of here. Captain Steele and a couple others are coming for me as soon as possible. They're taking me to Petra!"

"That's great news."

Chang told Judd what had happened at the palace during the last few hours, and Judd relayed his story about the guards and the building they raided.

"You're right in the thick of things," Chang said. "There's supposed to be some kind of emergency meeting there tomorrow morning. Nicolae was supposed to come, but with the plague of darkness, I'm not sure."

"We're following a lead on a concentration camp," Judd said.

"I've felt so bad that I haven't been able to do much about that. I've tried to slow things down with shipments and computer glitches, but they've even constructed a camp here on an island."

"Is there any way to tell if the darkness has affected it?"

"I'm sure it has, but let me check. Look, you and your friend must come with us to Petra."

"Right," Judd said. "Get back with the time of the flight as soon as you know."

Judd started to dial Vicki to give her the good news, but Zvi tapped on the window. "I think I'm ready."

"You are?"

"I've actually read Dr. Ben-Judah's Web site more than once. When he came on television and said that all the prophecies pointed to Jesus of Nazareth as Messiah, I laughed. My whole family scoffed at his statement. But God brought back much of what he said while you were talking. I can't believe I've been so blind."

"You can give your life to God right now and live for him the rest of your life."

"That's what I want to do."

"I'll pray with you."

"Yes, please."

"God, I thank you for my new friend, and right now we come to you with grateful hearts that you've helped us live through these terrible days. And I thank you that you've called Zvi to be your child."

Zvi picked up the prayer. "Lord God, I'm sorry for rejecting you and your Son for so long. I know that I've sinned and I've gone my own way. But now I want to choose your path. I believe Jesus died for me, that he was the Lamb of God—I just remembered that from Dr. Ben-Judah. You are the Lamb who took my sins and paid my debt. And I believe you did rise from the dead, not like Carpathia, but you came back to give life. Lord God, change me. Help me to live for you. Help me to tell others about you and follow you for the rest of my days."

"Amen," Judd said.

"Yes, amen."

Zvi opened his eyes and gasped. "I can see! I can finally see!"

NINE

The Meeting

AFTER Judd gave Westin and Gunther the good news about Zvi, the group rejoiced. Judd also told them about the meeting the next morning.

"I'd like to sit in on that," Gunther said.

Westin smiled. "No reason we can't."

It was late and everyone was tired. Westin suggested they backtrack to a hotel he had seen on the way and get some sleep.

While they drove to the hotel, Judd phoned Vicki and explained what had happened. She was overjoyed that Judd was safe and that they had helped a new believer, but she hesitated when Judd told her about the meeting the next morning.

"Why aren't you trying to get out of there?" Vicki said.

"Vick, listen—"

"No, you don't seem to care about what I think."

"I do care. It's just that it's so clear. I don't know why God has turned out the lights in New Babylon. I don't understand everything about the prophecies. But I do know that we might have a chance to save a bunch of lives and help them come to know God."

Vicki was silent on the other end.

"Vick, put yourself in my place."

"I'm trying."

"This doesn't mean I love you any less. And your support means so much."

"I'll pray. I can do that much. But I can't hide the fact that I'm ticked at you."

"Ticked at me, or ticked that God would put me in this place?"

Vicki paused. "I guess I'm ticked at both you and God."

"Then I'm in good company."

Vicki chuckled and sighed. "Be careful, Judd."

"I love you."

Judd's car was the last of the group to pull up to the hotel. New Babylon was half ghost town, half freak show. There were people on the street, crying and moaning, looking for some relief from their pain. Others seemed to have hidden away.

Westin grabbed Judd, and they ran to the

hotel office. "We need a bunch of rooms. Okay if I put Zvi with you?"

"Sure," Judd said.

The lobby of the hotel was plush, with thick leather chairs and expensive rugs. Westin stepped to the front desk, looked around, then vaulted it with one leap. He rubbed his hands together. "Let's get some rooms."

"What do you think you're doing?" a Middle Eastern man said. Judd turned and saw a nicely dressed man in a doorway by the front desk. His eyes were wild. "Who are you?"

"Sir, we're with the Global Community," Westin said. "There's a big meeting tomorrow morning near here, and we need a few hours of sleep."

The manager sighed with relief. "And you are able to see?"

"Special optical lenses. It's another one of those solar things. The potentate anticipated this, but we weren't able to outfit the population. Hopefully we'll be handing these out if the darkness continues."

A look of hope came over the man and he walked forward. "I was afraid this was some kind of . . . well, let me try to help you. We have many guests. How many rooms do you need?"

Westin told him.

"I can't see the computer, but most of our top floor is empty. If I gave you a master key . . ."

"That would be fine. We'll just slip in and get some rest and be gone by morning. When the lights come back on you can bill us."

"We have had many GC guests stay with us in the past."

"Good. Then you know the billing procedure."

The man hesitated.

"What's wrong?" Westin said.

"Nothing. It's just that you don't sound like any Peacekeepers I know."

"No, we're actually escaped Judah-ites from the local facility."

The manager laughed. "Yes, I suppose if you weren't GC, you wouldn't be staying here. And you wouldn't have those special lenses to help you see."

The man gave Westin two master keys, and Judd helped lead the group quietly to the elevators.

Judd had never seen such luxurious rooms. The room he and Zvi found was so big it even had a grand piano in it. A television screen took up most of one wall.

Judd fell asleep quickly and minutes later,

or so it seemed, Westin and Gunther were standing over him, telling him to wake up.

"You've got time for a quick shower," Westin said.

Judd showered, dressed, and met them downstairs where the same manager was still on duty. They tiptoed out the entrance and headed for the meeting.

Something had bothered Judd about Westin since they had teamed up to rescue the people in the Indiana library. He seemed to have no problem lying to the GC or to members of the Tribulation Force. Judd tried to bring up the subject.

Westin frowned. "Look, this is war. Life or death. These people will chop our heads off. And pretty soon they'll be gunning for us with nukes."

"The GC is one thing, but to lie to Rayford Steele about me—"

"I was trying to do you a favor and keep you out of trouble."

"I know, and I'm grateful you wanted to look out for me—"

"Then drop it. If you have a problem with it, let me go my way and you go yours."

Judd felt frustrated that the conversation had turned into a fight, but he still felt bad about Westin's lies.

Gunther got them focused on the task ahead and explained that the meeting would most likely be in the first floor conference room they had passed the night before.

Not wanting to arouse suspicion, they parked a few blocks away and headed for the facility on foot. The streets looked the same as the night before. They passed several bodies. Those who were alive were in agony.

The ones who could walk looked like they were drunk, tipping one way, then the other. Judd noticed one man walking quickly toward a building, heading straight for a descending stairway. Judd called out, but it was too late. The man fell like a rag doll to the bottom. Judd shouted and raced down the stairs.

"Who is that?" someone said behind him. "Are you with the Global Community?"

Judd kept quiet and felt the man's neck for a pulse but found none. He guessed the man had broken his neck on the way down.

Then he heard it.

The sound began as a soft, crackling noise wafting through the streets. As Judd reached the top of the steps he made out the strains of a recorded version of "Hail Carpathia," sung by the 500-voice Carpathianism Chorale:

Hail Carpathia, our lord and risen king;
Hail Carpathia, rules o'er everything.
We'll worship him until we die;
He's our beloved Nicolae.
Hail Carpathia, our lord and risen king.

Judd's stomach turned when he heard the
song. Then a voice Judd didn't recognize
came over the loudspeakers. The man
sounded like he was in pain as he said,
"Loyal subjects of the Global Community,
please move toward the sound you're hearing
for food and water. We have a supply station
nearby where you can find rations.

"Also, for those attending the joint staff
meeting, please come to the aid station and
move directly up the stairs to the conference
room. The meeting will begin in ten
minutes."

Westin came up beside Judd. "You notice
anything about these people?"

"They're in a lot of pain," Judd said.

"Yeah, but they're not singing along.
Usually they'd be chirping with the choir,
praising Carpathia."

Westin was right. Some were even grum-
bling against the potentate. "Carpathia's
always told people the big advantage of
worshiping him was that he was a god you

could see," Westin said. "I guess the real God took care of that for a while."

Judd found the aid station, which was a couple of tables set up with water bottles and premade sandwiches. Those who found the tables grabbed food and ate hungrily.

Others cried out in the distance. "What's happening here? Why can't we see?"

"How long will this darkness last?"

"Why am I in such pain?"

The aid workers, who were GC Peacekeepers pulled into service, were in just as bad of shape as those on the street. They had no answers.

No one blocked Judd's path as he walked up the steps. He passed a man in uniform crawling. The man had several stars on his shoulders, and medals clinked against the steps.

Gunther motioned them silently past an armed Peacekeeper. The Peacekeeper clutched his stomach and was nearly doubled over in pain. Despite his anguish, he repeated a phrase every few seconds. "Only authorized GC personnel past this point. Joint Chiefs meet directly across the hall."

Judd moved to the conference room where several people sipped at water bottles and moaned. Judd, Westin, and Gunther spread out around the room.

The man who had been crawling walked into the room, stopped, and announced, "General Showalter!"

The people around the table tried to stand and salute, but only half of them could make it out of their chairs. Judd wondered what difference it made, since none of them could see each other.

The general staggered to the table and sat.

The others collapsed in their chairs, and a woman pushed a weird-looking phone forward. "Chief Akbar wants us to call as soon as the meeting begins."

"Yes, I know. The potentate won't be here?"

"In this blackness?" a man to his right said. "We're lucky to have found our way from only a few blocks away."

The general punched the numbers slowly, and Judd recognized Suhail Akbar's voice on the speakerphone.

"Chief Akbar, can you give us an update on the situation?" the general said.

"I just returned from a meeting with the potentate. It appears that he is the only one we've found who can see in this most recent . . . phenomenon. You'll be pleased to know his presence actually provides a glow."

"How much of a glow?"

"Only about three feet around him, but it is quite comforting to know he has this situation under control. You will be encouraged to know that New Babylon is, at the moment, the only area affected by this blackout. Other countries have reported no loss of light, so it appears this is an isolated incident."

"Does anyone at the palace know why this happened?" someone said.

Akbar paused. "It may be a side effect of the heat wave, or it could be another electro-magnetic phenomenon. No matter what the cause, the potentate assures us that it will pass very soon."

"Does the potentate know about the suicides?" another man said. "We can't work in this cursed darkness. It took me two hours just to find my way here, and it's only a ten-minute walk. And the pain. Are we to believe the pain we feel is caused by leftover effects of the sun?"

"I understand your concerns, and believe me, everyone at the palace is doing their best to provide relief. We are using your idea of loudspeakers here near the palace and should have a message from the Most High Reverend Father to calm the fears of those who have been affected."

Akbar cleared his throat. "The current concern is with the Island facility. As you know, the potentate has considered closing this, and now he is anxious about the prisoners there."

"Why is he anxious?" the general said.

"The Island is the only camp for Jews in the blacked-out area. He is requesting that you go ahead with extermination plans of all prisoners immediately."

Judd glanced at Westin and Gunther who both looked horrified.

"How do you propose we do that since we can't even see the prisoners?" a man in front of Judd said.

"We have every confidence that you will find a way. Shoot them. Gas them. Burn them. The potentate doesn't care how you accomplish this, just that it gets done."

"If that is the potentate's wish, we shall oblige," the general said. "We will communicate with the guards there and inform them of our plan."

The phone clicked and went dead. The general dialed the number again, but there was no response. Judd noticed Gunther had knelt and was doing something at the wall. He motioned for Judd and Westin and held up the phone cord he had pulled from the wall. Then he held up his cell phone and pointed toward the group at the table.

He wants us to take all the cell phones! Judd thought.

Judd moved to the end of the room and began collecting the phones placed on the table.

There was a flurry of activity in the room as they tried to get Akbar back on the line.

"Someone just took my cell phone," a woman said.

"Mine's gone too," a man shouted.

Gunther motioned to the door, and Judd and Westin moved quickly toward it. The general dialed his cell phone, but before Suhail Akbar answered, Gunther grabbed the phone from the general. Gunther raced outside and closed the door. "Terribly sorry about the technical difficulty, Chief Akbar. We'll get on the Island operation right away."

"Good," Akbar said as Gunther held the phone out for Judd to hear. "I'll inform the potentate that this matter will be cared for today."

"It certainly will," Gunther said.

The Island

WHILE Westin returned to the hotel, Judd and Gunther blocked the conference room door. The general screamed and two Peacekeepers came fumbling toward them, their guns raised, but Gunther disarmed them quickly and sent them running.

Gunther returned with a hammer, nails, and blocks of wood he had found in a workshop area. "That should give us some time."

Judd followed Gunther to an electrical box a floor below, and the two spent a few minutes tearing out all of the phone wires. When they were through, they raced upstairs and locked the front door. A crowd had gathered at the aid station below as people pushed and jockeyed for food and water.

An hour later Westin returned, and Judd squeezed into a squad car with Gunther and the others headed for the Island. Judd dialed Chang Wong and told him their plan.

"I support your efforts," Chang said, "but I'm worried you won't get back in time for our flight to Petra. Captain Steele is on his way now."

"I'll have to take my chances," Judd said. "This mission we're on is a matter of life and death."

Gunther made a phone call of his own, informing their other contact in New Babylon, Otto Weser, about the deaths of Rainer and Klaus. Judd could tell Gunther was trying to smooth over the rift the group had had with Otto.

"Let us know when you and the others are planning to get out of here," Gunther said.

Because of the distance to the Island and the fact that they had to drive so slowly, it took them a few hours to make it to the concentration camp. They drove by an open field, and Judd noticed towers that seemed to reach into the sky. "Is this thing surrounded by razor wire?"

Gunther stopped the car, stepped out, and picked up a stick. "Worse than that. Watch."

He heaved the stick toward the field and it stopped in midair, sizzling, crackling, and falling to the ground.

"It's a new kind of electric fence. Anyone

who runs past the checkpoints and heads for this thing is toast."

"So there's only one way in?" Judd said.

Gunther nodded. "And one way out."

The car stopped and the group got out. Zvi asked to join the rescue since he had known some of the men inside.

Gunther pursed his lips and nodded. "First we go in and disarm the guards. Hopefully they know nothing about the order from Carpathia. Stay calm and let me do the talking."

Judd's heart pounded like a freight train as he and the others quietly walked the perimeter to the front gate. Two guards, one tall and lanky, the other shorter and smoking a cigarette, stood near the gate.

"Wonder when our relief will get here," the tall one said, scratching his head. "I can't see my watch, but we've had to have been here more than eight hours."

"I don't know how they can expect us to work in this," the shorter one moaned.

"Attention!" Gunther yelled.

One guard pointed his rifle toward Gunther's voice, and the other stood straight.

"General Showalter and his group are here for the inspection. You did get the message from the palace, did you not?" Gunther shoved an ID card into the man's hand and the guard looked down, a puzzled look on his face.

"We haven't heard a thing, sir," the short one said, flinging his cigarette to the ground. Judd wondered how the man had lit it without being able to see the flame. "We've had some communication problems, General, my apology."

Westin took up the ruse and lowered his voice. "I understand. You boys are doing a good job out here." He patted the short one on the back. "Prisoners are still here, right? You haven't let them get away?"

"No, sir," the short one said. "We've been right here all night . . . or day. Whichever. I can't tell anymore." He paused. "Uh, sir, are you able to see?"

"New goggles," Westin said. "We should have a shipment for you in a day or two."

"Where's the motor pool?" Gunther said. "You still have transport vehicles here, right?"

"Yes, sir," the tall one said. He started to point, then bit his lip. "They're at the north end of the compound. Outside the fence."

"Good," Gunther said, grabbing a radio from the guard shack. "Radio us immediately if there's any kind of problem."

"Yes, sir," the tall one said. "Do you want us to notify—?"

"No, this is a surprise inspection. Not a word to anyone."

"Yes, sir. Not a word, sir."

"You, come with us," Westin said.

"Me, sir?" the short one said.

"Yes. We'll need you to show us around."

"But, sir, I can't see."

"No problem. Just give me your gun so you don't trip and kill us all, and tell me where to go."

Judd squeezed past the other guard and followed Westin, Gunther, and the guard down the paved road that led to the prison. Zvi followed.

The entrance to the camp was a looming, creepy archway with a likeness of Nicolae carved into it. Climbing up a few steps, they faced a series of doors.

"How do we get inside without announcing our arrival?" Westin said.

"I can use my key, sir," the guard said.

"Let me have it," Gunther said.

He put the key in and the doors clicked. A few paces and they were inside. "Looks like your friends in here aren't as alert as you are," Gunther said.

"The others are probably near the prisoners, sir."

"Take us to them. Are they all in one area?"

"The cells run in a horseshoe shape around
the outside of the building. In the middle is
the common area where the prisoners are
now. And then there's the . . . well . . ."

"The torture area?" Westin said. "Come on,
man. You're not used to that yet?"

"No, sir, I can't get used to the screaming.
That's one reason why they put me outside."

"Take us to this common area then,"
Westin barked.

The guard told them which way to go, and
Westin and Gunther led the way. As far as
Judd knew, the guard didn't know he and Zvi
were there.

Through thick Plexiglas, Judd spotted the
common area. There were no chairs or
benches, basketball hoops, or anything he
would have normally thought of as being in
a prison yard. It was simply an area filled
with dirt. Men stood leaning against the
building, some lying down. He noticed some
scratching and moaning in pain.

With Westin's help, the guard led them
down a flight of stairs and through a security
area. Two more guards stopped them.

Westin put on his General Showalter act
again. "I want you to round up all the guards

who are inside and have them meet us in the torture room."

"Yes, sir."

Within ten minutes all the guards had gathered near a door. At Westin's request they put their guns down outside the room and went inside. Judd couldn't believe how easily the men gave up their weapons.

When Westin had the door locked, they went into the common area and walked through the prisoners. Judd saw no one with the mark of the believer and only a few with the mark of Carpathia.

Gunther turned to Judd. "You did such a good job with Zvi, I'm going to give you the opportunity to speak with these men."

"Me?" Judd said.

"Westin and I are going to try and get the juice turned off on that electric fence. Gather them up and do your thing."

＊

Vicki awoke and looked around the room. They were back to sleeping during the day and staying up at night, and Vicki hadn't adjusted yet. She had finally fallen asleep after her conversation with Judd, but now she was wide awake.

The first person who came to mind was

Chloe Williams. Odd. With Judd in New Babylon and going into such a dangerous situation, why would she think of Chloe? Was God trying to tell her something?

She lay back on her bed and tried to get to sleep, but Chloe's face kept coming to mind. Vicki prayed for her, for little Kenny, for Buck, and for the others who were living underground in San Diego.

Before she fell asleep, she prayed again that Judd would receive wisdom from God about what to do in New Babylon.

✤

"Gentlemen, if I could have your attention," Judd yelled. He had moved to the end of the horseshoe-shaped area. Zvi stood nearby. "Walk toward me. I have something important to say."

The men hobbled forward, some tripping over those on the ground. A few fell to the ground and crawled. Judd wondered how these men had kept from being burned during the heat wave. Most looked like walking skeletons, with hair falling out, and wearing ragged clothes.

"What will you do to us next?" a toothless man shouted. "Haven't you tortured us enough?"

"I'm not here to torture you," Judd said. "I come with good news. Your cries have been heard. This day you will have your freedom."

The men stared into the darkness, unable to understand what Judd was saying.

Finally, the toothless man spoke again. "Do you mean you will finally let us die?"

Judd took a breath. "My friends and I aren't with the Global Community. We heard about your struggle and have taken advantage of the plague of darkness. We come to offer you sight, both physical and spiritual."

A murmur rose from the gathering. Some didn't believe Judd and thought it was another GC trick. "They're going to kill us all!" a man said.

"That's what you've been begging them to do for weeks," another said. "Shut up and listen."

"The God of Abraham, Isaac, and Jacob has caused this blackout," Judd continued. "He foretold this day in his holy Word, warning people about the leader who would rise and come against his people, the Jews. That leader is Nicolae Carpathia, and he's persecuting you because of your Jewish blood.

"God caused everything from the disappearances, to the earthquake, to the stinging locusts, and all the rest, including this plague. It's one of his final acts to get you to repent of your sins and come to him through his Son, the Messiah."

"This is another Judah-ite!" a man yelled. "We've had your kind in our midst before, trying to get us to pray to Jesus."

"We don't want your religion," the toothless man said, turning his back.

"Listen to me," Judd screamed. The men calmed as the hum of the electric fence shut off. "This may be your last chance. We are trying to get people to safety, but we won't force you. If you want to hear more about the God who loves you and gave his life for you, please stay. We'll provide you with food and shelter and safe passage to Petra when we can."

"And if we don't want to listen?"

"You're free to go," Judd shouted. "But I beg you not to squander this chance."

To Judd's astonishment, hundreds of men scurried forward past him. They clawed at each other, cursed and spat upon those who fell in their way, and rushed away in a panic.

When he turned back, only forty or fifty remained. Judd wondered how many of these were simply too scared to walk into the darkness.

Judd gave the same message he had heard from Tsion Ben-Judah and Bruce Barnes. It was the same one he had seen transform old and young alike. He spoke of the prophecies that foretold the coming of the Messiah and how Jesus had fulfilled these verses. His heart welled up as he looked at the gaunt faces of the men.

Zvi stepped forward and told his story. Before he had finished, several men asked, "What do we have to do?"

Judd led them in a prayer, much like the one he had prayed with Zvi the day before. Several received the mark of the believer. They were shaking hands with each other, slapping each other's backs, and praising God. Others who stood nearby asked why they were so happy, and the men told them they could see.

Westin walked up to Judd and pointed to the transport trucks. Judd told the new believers to follow Westin and said if any more were interested, they should grab on to him and follow. Like a winding kindergarten group, the men trudged through the darkness clinging to Judd.

If only Vicki could see this, Judd thought.

ELEVEN

Bad News
in San Diego

JUDD stared at the odd mix of believers in the parking lot of the hotel. It was morning and they were all together now. Those who weren't believers when they left the prison had since become convinced of the claims of Jesus. Judd wandered through the group while they ate breakfast or rested, catching the smiles of the men he had helped.

Westin and Gunther knelt together by the front of the transport truck. Judd walked up as Gunther patted Westin on the shoulder. "It's decided then."

"What's decided?" Judd said.

"We're going to take advantage of this new manpower and put the Global Community on its heels," Gunther said.

"What are you talking about?" Judd said.

"We have to get back to the airport and get to Petra."

Gunther stood and put an arm on Judd's shoulder. "I understand, but we have pressing matters here."

Westin stood. "There are a lot more guillotines to destroy, and if we can get in Nicolae's palace before this darkness lifts—"

"But you can't do that," Judd said. "You might destroy valuable stuff the Trib Force needs."

"I don't understand," Gunther said.

"We've had a guy on the inside for a long time, giving us information. You destroy their computer network and you've hurt the GC for maybe a week. But you'll cripple the Trib Force's efforts to know what's going on."

"I had no idea there was someone on the inside," Gunther said.

Judd looked at his watch. "And he's supposed to fly out of here sometime today."

Westin pursed his lips. "I still like the idea of staying and doing as much harm as we can while the lights are out."

"Agreed," Gunther said.

Judd rubbed his eyes and sighed. This trip to New Babylon was supposed to have been quick, in and out, but here he was, days after he had first arrived. He had helped men escape the clutches of the GC, and some had become believers, but he couldn't help thinking about the safety of Petra.

"I understand your need to get to Petra," Westin said. "If you want to head to the airport, I'll help."

Judd hadn't talked with Chang since the day before and wondered how he was doing. He pulled out his cell phone and dialed as a rumble shattered the darkness.

"Who could be flying an airplane in this darkness?" Gunther said.

Judd's heart sank. "Rayford Steele."

Chang picked up on the second ring, and Judd asked him where he was.

"We just took off from New Babylon. And you should have seen Nicolae."

"He was at the airport?"

"Yes, and believe it or not, there's a glow about him."

"So you're headed to Petra?" Judd said.

"We had to get out of here. I haven't had a chance to tell Captain Steele about your situation. Where are you?"

Judd told him and Chang groaned. "I know that hotel. We could have waited another few minutes, I suppose, but not long enough for you to reach us. What happened at the concentration camp?"

Judd told him and Chang was overjoyed.

He finally handed the phone to Rayford Steele, and Judd told the pilot what had happened over the past few days.

"Looks like you have two options, Judd," Rayford said. "You can find our contact there—his name is Otto Weser—and wait for the next airlift out, or you can hop in that truck and head across the desert. Both scenarios have their problems."

"I understand," Judd said. "Did you learn anything in New Babylon?"

"Plenty," Rayford said. "I made a contact inside the palace, met this Otto character, and we crashed a meeting of Carpathia's."

"You were actually in the room with Nicolae?"

"He didn't know we were there, but yes. We overheard him telling his people he's going to put an end to the 'Jewish problem' and he's calling a meeting of all ten heads of the global regions. They're going to meet in Baghdad to map out their strategy. And we found out Nicolae's storehouse of nuclear weapons is hidden at Al Hillah."

"The nukes the world gave up and he was supposed to destroy?"

"Right. He's moving his operation there, though the palace will still hold his staff." Rayford's phone chirped. "I've got a call from

San Diego. I'd better take this. Take care, Judd. Hope to see you in Petra soon."

"Me too," Judd said.

※

Vicki knew Judd was trying to put a good face on the situation, but she could tell he was disappointed to still be in New Babylon.

"I feel like I've failed you," Judd said. "I promised I'd be careful, and I'm still in one of the most dangerous spots in the world."

"Not if this is what God wants," Vicki said. "I'm disappointed too, but look how God's used you. We've prayed that we could reach more people, and that's what happened."

"We've made the decision to find this German guy, Otto Weser. Our group and Otto's separated because of a disagreement, but maybe we'll all get out of this and get to Petra."

Vicki kept her composure until after she was off the phone with Judd. Then she ran to her cabin, buried her face in her pillow, and wept.

※

Two days later Vicki found herself among her friends, praying for Judd and asking God to protect him and the other believers in New Babylon. Judd had called twice and updated her on their progress. They had found Otto Weser and what Judd termed a safe place to stay and perform their operations against the GC. Judd also said they had an option of driving into the desert to hide, but that for the moment they were staying in New Babylon.

What happened next took Vicki's breath away. Mark was monitoring different news feeds and came upon Anika Janssen anchoring live from Detroit. "On the preview they mentioned something about an important arrest," Mark said.

"Where?" Vicki said.

Mark pointed at the screen and turned up the volume.

"Good evening," Anika Janssen said. "Darkness continues to plague Global Community International Headquarters in New Babylon at this hour. It is confined to the borders of the city and is believed to be an act of aggression on the part of dissidents against the New World Order.

"GC Chief of Security and Intelligence Suhail Akbar spoke with us by phone earlier from the beleaguered capital. In spite of the turmoil there, he reports good news, constituting our top story tonight."

The screen showed an outline of the New Babylon skyline and a picture of Suhail

Akbar. "Yes, Anika," Akbar said, "following months of careful planning and cooperation between the various law-enforcement branches of the Global Community, we are happy to report that a combined task force of crack agents from both our Peacekeeping and Morale Monitor divisions has succeeded in apprehending one of the top Judah-ite terrorists in the world.

"The arrest was made before dawn today in San Diego after months of planning."

"San Diego!" Vicki said.

"I'd rather not go into the details of the operation," Akbar continued, "but the suspect was disarmed and arrested without incident. Her name is Chloe Steele Williams, twenty-six, a former campus radical at Stanford University in Palo Alto, California, from which she was expelled six years ago after making threats on the lives of the administration."

"Thank you, Chief Akbar. We have further learned that Mrs. Williams is the daughter of Rayford Steele, who once served as pilot for Global Community Supreme Potentate Nicolae Carpathia. He was fired some years ago for insubordination and drinking while on duty, and GC intelligence believes his resentment led to his current role as an international terrorist."

"I don't believe this," Mark said. "Those are such lies!"

"Mrs. Williams is the wife of Cameron Williams, formerly a celebrated American journalist who also worked directly for the potentate before losing his job due to differences in management style. He edits a subversive cyber and printed magazine with a limited circulation.

"Williams, his wife, and her father are international fugitives in exile, wanted for more than three dozen murders around the world. Mrs. Williams herself heads a black-market operation suspected of hijacking billions of Nicks' worth of goods around the world and selling them for obscene profits to others who cannot legally buy and sell due to their refusal to pledge loyalty to the potentate.

"The Williamses, who have amassed a fortune on the black market, have one child remaining after Mrs. Williams apparently aborted two fetuses and an older daughter died under questionable circumstances. The son, whom they have named Jesus Savior Williams, pictured here, is two years old. Acquaintances report that the Williamses believe he is the reincarnation of Jesus Christ, who will one day conquer Nicolae Carpathia and return the globe to Christianity."

The screen filled with a picture of a toddler wearing a T-shirt that read "Kill Carpathia!"

"That can't be Kenny," Vicki said.

"There are so many lies in that report," Conrad said, "I wouldn't be surprised if Carpathia wrote it himself."

"Do you think they really arrested Chloe?" Vicki said.

Mark held up a hand as the report switched to a reporter in San Diego who stood by the man who was said to be interrogating Chloe.

Colonel Jonathan "Jock" Ashmore said the arrest was very important. He nervously tugged at his uniform jacket. "Mrs. Williams has proved to be the typical terrorist who knows when it's time to bargain. When the reality hit her that she had been positively identified and we informed her of the overwhelming charges against her, it was only a matter of minutes before she began offering various deals to save her skin."

"Are you at liberty to say what some of those might be?"

"Not entirely, though she has already

pledged to enroll her son in Junior GC as
soon as possible."

"I've seen enough," Vicki said. "There's no
way Chloe would have talked, and there's
certainly no way she would have agreed to
enroll Kenny in a Junior GC program."

Vicki walked away from the video feed,
shaken and confused. She pictured Chloe
being tortured and questioned by her GC
captors.

In a response written to Dr. Ben-Judah's
Web site, Mark received the answers the
people in Petra were sending out to counteract the lies of the GC.

> The only thing the news seemed to get
> right was Chloe's name and age and the
> fact that she is the daughter of Rayford
> and the wife of Cameron "Buck"
> Williams. While it's true she attended
> Stanford University, neither was she a
> campus radical nor was she expelled. She
> dropped out after the Rapture but had a
> grade point average of 3.4 and had been
> active in student affairs.
>
> Rayford Steele did serve, while already
> a believer, as pilot on the staff of Nicolae
> Carpathia, providing invaluable informa-
> tion to the cause of Christ's followers
> everywhere. He was never fired and never

charged with insubordination or drinking while on duty. He left after his second wife was killed in a plane crash.

The Judah-ites are anything but "the ast holdouts in opposition to the New World Order." Many Jewish and Muslim factions, as well as former militia groups primarily in the United North American States, still have refused to accept the mark of loyalty to the Supreme Potentate and must hide in fear for their lives.

Cameron Williams was indeed formerly a celebrated American journalist who also worked directly for the potentate, but he also quit, rather than "losing his job due to differences in management style." As for his subversive cyber and printed magazine's "limited circulation," that, of course, is a matter of opinion. The Truth is circulated to the same audience that is ministered to daily by Dr. Tsion Ben-Judah, at last count still more than a billion.

The rest of the document corrected errors from the GC about murders, the Co-op, and Chloe's personal life.

"That clears up her past," Vicki said, "but what are they going to do with her?"

Mark pursed his lips. "If she could stay alive for another year, she'd be around for the Glorious Appearing. But I honestly don't think that'll happen."

Judd reeled from the news reports about Chloe and put a call in to Chang in Petra. He was surprised to hear excitement in Chang's voice when he got the return call.

"I know it's a very depressing day for the Tribulation Force around the world," Chang said, "but I have good news. I'm free."

"Right, you made it to Petra. I'm happy for you."

"No, you don't understand. The mark on my forehead. It is gone!"

TWELVE

The Missing Mark

JUDD fought feelings of jealousy, wishing he were in Petra with Chang, but the news that his mark was gone was incredible. Judd knew how much Carpathia's mark bothered Chang, and he couldn't imagine the embarrassment of walking into that camp of a million people with the emblem of the enemy on his forehead.

"I thought Nicolae's tattoo was permanent," Judd said. "What happened?"

"I arrived here in the afternoon, and Naomi Tiberius gave me a quick tour, including the computer center," Chang said. "It's amazing what Mr. Hassid set up. It's just like being in New Babylon without the danger."

"Everyone treating you okay?"

"Like royalty. But I'm so ashamed. I wanted to take off my baseball cap and bow every time I met someone new, but with that thing on my forehead, I could not."

"Did you meet Tsion and Chaim?"

"Yes, but not right away. They were meeting about Chloe's disappearance, and then came the news of another Tribulation Force member's death."

"Who?"

"Albie. A man Captain Steele and the others know well. The GC reported that Chloe gave up information about him, but no one believes that. And they say he committed suicide, which, again, no one believes."

Judd hadn't heard of this Albie, but if he was a member of the Trib Force, Judd knew he would be missed. "I want to hear more about your mark, but how's Captain Steele?"

"As well as can be expected. He left here not long after we arrived. He received a call from Chloe from a GC cell phone, and she gave him a coded message. I don't know all the particulars, but Captain Steele believes she was trying to tell him to get everyone in San Diego to Petra, and that's what he's trying to work out."

"Seems like the safest place to be," Judd said.

Chang described his new home. Again, Judd felt a stirring in his heart, wishing he were in Petra talking with Chang and eating manna or quail.

"How did you like the manna?" Judd said.

"It was like being fed from the table of a king. That's how a friend described it and he was right. Naomi gave me a tour on one of the ATVs. The city is so spread out that it would take days to see everything."

"Is something going on between you and Naomi?"

Chang paused. "We have a good relationship. I knew we would have to work together closely since she has become the technical leader here, but I didn't want to complicate things with . . ."

"You're falling for her, aren't you?"

"Judd, she is stunning—"

"I know. I've met her. Friendly, beautiful, and smarter than both of us."

"I've never even had a girlfriend. There were girls in high school I was interested in, but I never dared let them know."

"Do you think she feels anything for you?"

Chang chuckled. "I think so. We were drinking at the spring of water when the sun set and the skies opened and seemed to snow bits of soft bread."

Judd closed his eyes and pictured the scene. It was one of the most amazing things he had witnessed in Petra, the daily food that fell from the sky, as if God were tearing off pieces of bread and sending them floating to his children.

"Talking with Naomi is like speaking with someone I've known my whole life, but I've never met her in person. Do you understand?"

"I do."

"Anyway, I met her father, which was quite an experience, and then I met with Tsion and Chaim. We are all heartbroken about Chloe."

"They must be trying to help her escape," Judd said.

"I don't know. That will be up to Captain Steele and Mr. Williams."

"I can't imagine what Buck is going through right now. Tell me about the mark."

"Yes. I met Dr. Rosenzweig, who looks more like his old self now than the famous Micah who stood up to the potentate. His hair's grown back and he was excited to see me. He called me 'the genius mole.'

"Then Dr. Ben-Judah approached with all kinds of people around him. I was honored he would eat a short breakfast with me. When he prayed over our meal, I thought my heart was going to burst. After our meal, I asked for some time alone with him and Dr. Ben-Judah stayed.

"I took off my cap and showed him the 30 on my forehead and the place where the Global Community biochip had been inserted. He said it was strange to see both the mark of the believer *and* the mark of Carpathia, and I told him I couldn't stand to look myself in the mirror each day."

"That mark kept you alive, Chang," Judd said.

"Yes, Tsion said it wasn't my fault, that it was forced on me, but I asked if there was any way to have it gone.

"Tsion scratched his chin and shrugged. He said he didn't know if it was possible, but that he would pray, as long as I would be content with whatever God decided."

"What happened then?"

"He called Naomi's father and Chaim back over to agree with us in prayer. I was already overcome with emotion and had begun to cry. Tsion placed his hand on my forehead, and the others grabbed my hands and touched my shoulders. I felt so loved by these men, so cared for. And then Tsion prayed. It was such a beautiful prayer that included many Scriptures.

"The tears were streaming down my face as he turned to me. He said we come together in faith believing and pray to the God to whom anything is possible, the God who spared us from the fire of the enemy.

"And then he asked, according to God's will, if God would remove any sign of the evil one from me. I went limp. It felt like my arms and legs weighed a hundred pounds each. I started sweating like an Olympic athlete. I opened my eyes and Tsion looked at me and smiled.

"Naomi's father was the first to tell me it was gone. Then I ran to his place and looked in the mirror to make sure it was true. The mark no longer mocks me, Judd."

"I'm happy for you."

"We're gearing up for at least two hundred new arrivals here in the next few days, people from San Diego. When are you coming?"

Judd told him what had happened the last few days and what he hoped would happen. It was Judd's plan to get to Petra and have Vicki join him there if possible. "As long as it's dark over here, we're continuing to try and frustrate the GC as much as we can. I guess when the time's right, we'll head that way."

※

Vicki watched news reports from the Global Community and tried not to think about what Chloe was going through. Was she in some dark, cold cell? Were they torturing her, trying to get her to give information about the Tribulation Force? Vicki guessed the GC was having a hard time getting anything out of Chloe. She was one of the most determined people Vicki had ever met.

Chloe had set the Commodity Co-op in motion and had coordinated shipments of food and medical supplies for believers throughout the United North American States and the entire world. The GCNN reporters were right—the capture of Chloe was a tremendous success for the Global Community. But pulling information from her would be very difficult.

Vicki thought of her last conversation with Chloe. The woman had written to congratulate Vicki on her engagement. A few weeks later, Vicki had called Chloe in San Diego and talked with her about Judd's potential trip to New Babylon.

Chloe had been hesitant when Vicki told her about the trip. "Sounds like Buck to me," Chloe had said. "If there's something he can do to help the cause, he'll go there, no matter what the cost to him. But I have to admit I've done the same thing. In Greece I took some chances I wouldn't want Buck to take."

Chloe had talked about her son, Kenny,

during the conversation as well. "I just hope if anything happens to me or Buck that the other one will be there to help raise Kenny. I can't imagine not seeing him grow up."

The memory sent a chill down Vicki's spine as she reread a journal entry about some of the conversation. Vicki had written a prayer at the end of the page. *God, if anything does happen to Chloe or Buck, I pray that you would make it possible for me to help in some way to raise Kenny.*

The phone rang in the main cabin and Vicki was closest. Immediately she heard background noise like someone was on an airplane. "Hello?"

"Yes, I'm looking for Zeke—I'm not sure I have the right—"

"Captain Steele?" Vicki said.

"Yes, who's this?"

Vicki told him and asked Mark to get Zeke. "Where are you?" she said.

"We're flying over the southern states now, headed for home base. We came from Petra."

"I heard about Chloe. Is it true?"

"All the information we have points to them having her," Rayford said.

"We've been praying for her—and for you and Buck and Kenny."

Rayford cleared his throat. "That means more than you can know, Vicki. I was really excited for you and Judd. Have you heard any more from him?"

Vicki told him what she knew, and Rayford told her of his conversation with Judd earlier. "We have a contact who's still in New Babylon that we'll probably need to go in and get. If Judd's not out by then, maybe he can take that flight."

"That would be wonderful."

"Plus, I'm going to talk with Zeke about something that might help you as well. Do you sense much danger from the GC there in Wisconsin?"

"It's such a remote location, they seem to have forgotten us or don't really care that we're here."

Zeke rushed in so Vicki said good-bye to Rayford. Zeke took the phone in the other room and talked for a few minutes. He returned smiling.

"What did Captain Steele want?" Vicki said.

"He asked if I was ready to come out of mothballs."

Vicki raised an eyebrow. "What does that mean?"

"You know, come out of storage. Get in the game. Go where the action is. Seems they need some help in Petra and I'm on my way."

"What are you going to do there?"

Zeke frowned. "Don't know exactly. I figure I'll be working on disguises and such, you know, fake ID cards or uniforms or maybe some tattoos. Captain Steele didn't give specifics, but I told him if they needed me, I'd be there."

"I'm happy for you," Vicki said.

"You ought to be happy for yourself."

"What do you mean?"

Zeke sat in a rickety wooden chair that strained under his weight and smiled. "Because I'm supposed to have a little company on the flight."

"Who?"

"Well, the pilot will probably be Mac McCullum or whoever they assign, but there's a certain redheaded girl from Mount Prospect who's been given the okay to be on board as well."

"Me?" Vicki choked.

"And whoever you need for the ceremony once Judd makes it back," Zeke said.

Vicki covered her mouth, then waved a hand at her face. "I have to tell Lionel. He's supposed to be Judd's best man."

Zeke laughed. "Then go tell him."

THIRTEEN

Otto Weser

JUDD and a few others had moved into a
hideout run by Otto Weser less than six miles
from the GC palace. Westin had stayed with
Gunther and the rest of the group as they
tried to destroy Global Community guillotines and loyalty mark sites before the darkness ended.

After a long sleep, Judd finally met Otto.
The German timberman was barrel-chested,
with a wide grin and big hands. Judd asked
Otto only one question and the man was off,
talking a mile a minute and stopping for just
enough breath to continue. He told Judd he
had come to New Babylon to be part of the
fulfillment of prophecy that believers would
be called out of the city. Judd noticed he
didn't mention anything about the deaths of
Rainer's wife and the others.

"After the darkness plague hit, I knew what I had to do. For a long time I've wanted to see the palace with my own two eyes. So, when I couldn't convince anyone else to go with me, I went by myself to the compound, the courtyard, the palace—and I especially wanted to see Nicolae Carpathia's office."

"You actually went inside?" Judd said.

"Yes, and imagine my shock when I saw believers there. Four of them."

Judd quickly figured out that Otto had met Chang Wong, Rayford Steele, Abdullah Smith, and Naomi Tiberius.

"What an answer to prayer those people were. And to think, we have a connection in Petra when we need it."

When Otto took another breath, Judd said, "So you're not concerned about being here while Carpathia's goons are around?"

"Nicolae and his goons, as you call them, have left. Rayford Steele and I found out about a meeting in the palace and we went there. We actually saw Nicolae kill one of his top people. An Indian man, I think. Awful. Grabbed him with both hands and snapped his neck like a chicken bone. Then kept going with the meeting. Shows you what kind of man he is.

"Well, they reported a plane had landed, and Nicolae was personally going to inspect it. That was Rayford's plane so we had to get out of there, but before we did, we found out that Nicolae is calling together his ten kings, the leaders of all the global regions. That will happen in six months. But they're moving all leaders into the light at Al Hillah. That's where Nicolae has stored his nuclear weapons.

"Perhaps Nicolae just wants to be in the light, or perhaps he knows that New Babylon will be destroyed by God. I don't know. But one thing is certain. You and I are in a very strategic place, Mr. Judd Thompson Jr."

When Otto paused, Judd seized the opportunity. "I met Rainer. He told me a little about the disagreements you had."

Otto's face went white and he sighed. "You don't know how many times I've wished I could talk with him and tell him how sorry I was. I heard he and Klaus were killed, and I hold myself personally responsible." He put his hands on his knees. "Did Rainer ever say anything about me other than the story about his wife?"

Judd reached in his pocket and pulled out the letter Rainer had given him. Tears welled in the big man's eyes. He tore open the letter and quickly read the brief note. Otto shook with emotion, then folded the letter and put it in his shirt pocket. "I will never get to tell him how sorry I am."

"Yes, you will," Judd said. "You'll see each other again and the others."

"You're right. And that day is closer now than it has ever been."

After Judd finished talking with Otto, he spent some time praying for Chloe Williams. He didn't know much about the situation, but he knew enough to sense that she was in grave danger. He prayed the Tribulation Force would be able to rescue her and get out safely and that Chloe would stay strong and not give the GC any information.

Judd thought of Petra and remembered Sam Goldberg. It had been a while since they had talked, so he dialed the last number he had for the boy and reached the computer area at Petra.

After a few minutes, Sam was on the phone. "I've heard about your situation through Mr. Stein. He talked briefly with Captain Steele while he was here and got an update on you. We've been praying."

"How's it going with you?" Judd said.

"Let me step outside," Sam said quietly. "Most people prefer working inside at this time of day because it's hot." When he had moved outside, Sam said, "I'll be honest, Judd. I had feelings for Naomi."

"Did you talk with her?"

"Yes. She tried to let me down easy, but the truth is, my feelings haven't gone away. And now that Chang is here . . ."

"What's Chang got to do with it?"

"Naomi flew to New Babylon and has been with him almost every minute since they've been back. He's a genius with computers. I've watched him tapping into everything in New Babylon. He's not much older than me, and yet he's been given a major assignment by the Trib Force."

"You can understand that, though. The guy's been on the inside of the GC—"

"I know. And I can see why Naomi is attracted to him, but I'm still having . . ." Sam's voice trailed off. Then Judd heard him say hello to someone. "You won't believe who just walked by with a basket of manna for her sweetheart." Sam sighed. "With all the problems in the world, this one is so small."

"Sam, I'm really sorry. I'll pray that . . . well, I'll pray for you."

"I need it," Sam said.

With the turmoil of Judd's situation, plus learning about Chloe's capture, the last thing

Vicki needed was the emotional drain of saying good-bye. But here she was again, packing the few belongings she had and getting ready to leave the friends she had made over the past few years. She carefully folded and packed the wedding dress that several of the women had made for her. It was a comfort to know Lionel would be going along and Zeke would be there too, but she hated leaving.

A few hours before the trip to catch the Trib Force plane, the group gathered in the main cabin to bid farewell to their friends. Vicki cried when little Ryan walked up and handed her a picture of him and the Fogartys. On the back was written, *So you won't forget the joy you've brought our family.* Vicki hugged Ryan tightly and smiled through her tears at Tom and Josey.

Charlie brought Phoenix into the room, and the dog licked Vicki's face. "They say a dog is man's best friend," Charlie said, "but you've been mine, Vicki."

One by one they expressed their feelings for Vicki, Lionel, and Zeke. Darrion said she was thankful that Vicki was a person who knew how to listen. Janie, in her own way, gave tribute to Vicki and thanked her for sticking with her even when she didn't deserve it. Shelly couldn't speak. She just gave Vicki a long hug.

Mark tried to say something but couldn't. After what felt like ten minutes, but was really only one, he crossed his arms and leaned back in his chair. "I've known Vicki and Lionel as long as anyone here. We've had our disagreements, and some knock-down, drag-out fights." He looked at Vicki. "You were there when my cousin died. You've really been my family these last six years, and sometimes families get upset and bicker and . . ." He shook his head. "I don't know what to say other than . . . I love you."

Vicki, Lionel, and Mark hugged each other, the tears flowing.

Zeke blew his nose loudly and everyone laughed. "Sorry, but you guys are the ones making my nose run," he said.

When everyone had said something, Marshall Jameson stood. "It's been the treat of a lifetime getting to know you three. Zeke, you brought a servant's heart to this place. It's been an honor to serve alongside you. Lionel, you showed us what real courage is all about, and I pray God will use you in this last year as much as he's used you in our lives." Marshall paused and wiped away a tear. "And, Vicki, you have been a light. I couldn't be any happier for you and Judd, and I pray God will bless you both."

Marshall pulled out three handwritten notes. "I asked everyone to write something about you that you could take, something to remember us by. Some wrote verses that remind them of you, and others wrote personal things."

He handed them the three envelopes, then asked everyone to gather. Vicki, Zeke, and Lionel sat while the others put their hands on them.

"Oh, God, you have given us these friends who have blessed us with their lives. And now we give them back to you, asking that you will use them mightily. Watch over them and protect them. May they always remember the love we have for them and that our love is only a fraction of your love for them."

Marshall paused. There were sniffles and sobs all around Vicki. Finally he said, " 'And now, all glory to God, who is able to keep you from stumbling, and who will bring you into his glorious presence innocent of sin and with great joy. All glory to him, who alone is God our Savior, through Jesus Christ our Lord. Yes, glory, majesty, power, and authority belong to him, in the beginning, now, and forevermore. Amen.' "

An hour later, Marshall helped Zeke drag his boxes and trunks into the underbrush near Hudson, Wisconsin. They said good-bye again and Marshall was gone.

Vicki, Zeke, and Lionel stayed out of sight until they heard the whine of the jet engine overhead. Soon, Mac McCullum had touched down and was helping Zeke pull his things to the plane.

Mac was a tall, lanky man who talked with a drawl. Vicki had heard a lot about him from Judd and others who had met him. He had flown planes for the Global Community and was presumed dead when Nicolae's expensive jet crashed in Israel. Vicki recalled how glad she felt when she heard Mac had escaped the GC before the crash.

Mr. McCullum greeted Lionel and Vicki and showed them where to put their things. As they lugged Zeke's stuff, Mac asked about Zeke's stay in Wisconsin.

"I wish you could meet everybody in Avery," Zeke said.

"No second thoughts about leaving? You must be close to these people."

"Lots of second thoughts, but I figure a guy's got to go where he's called. I was called here, and now I'm being called there. Who woulda thought a no-account like me would ever get called anywhere?"

When they were in the air, Vicki got a good

look at the devastation from the heat wave. There were occasional patches of land that hadn't been affected, but most of the earth had been scorched. Cities looked like ghost towns.

Vicki asked about Chloe, and Mac told her what he knew. "We got a report in San Diego that Peacekeepers were coming our way, so we decided to get out fast. Most of us are heading to Petra, though I'm not sure if Rayford and Buck have made their final decision about a rescue."

"You mean they might not try?" Lionel said.

"Apparently they've moved Chloe to somewhere back east. We don't know where."

"Buck must be going out of his mind," Vicki said.

Mac pursed his lips. "And you should hear little Kenny crying for his mom. They're trying to take care of him, but nobody can do that like a mom can."

As Mac piloted them across the Atlantic, he told them what he knew about the Trib Force member named Albie who had been killed. "As much of this as we've gone through, it never gets easier. They're planning a little service for Albie at Petra once everybody gets there from San Diego."

Mac explained that he would drop them

off at Petra, then head to Al Basrah and clear his and Albie's apartment of any clues. "I'll be taking a bigger plane from Petra 'cause I got to bring back this Otto Weser guy and his people."

"Captain Steele told me about him," Zeke said. "So you're bringing them back to Petra because of that Scripture about God's people getting out of Babylon before God destroys it?"

"Exactly."

Vicki sat forward. "Do you think Judd will be in that group you bring from New Babylon?"

"If he's not, I'll find him and hog-tie him. We gotta get you two back together."

Zeke stared at the ocean seven and a half miles below. "What must that have looked like when it was all blood?"

"You can't imagine," Mac said.

Mac turned to Lionel and said he couldn't believe how Lionel had survived his ordeal in Indiana. "And it sounds like your time in South Carolina was no cakewalk."

Lionel told them what had happened to him during his travels and said he wondered if all those believers who had helped him on his way north were still alive.

Vicki tried to keep up with the conversation, but she fell asleep to the roar of the plane's engine. A new chapter was being written in her life, and this final year would begin in Petra.

FOURTEEN

The World Watches

W**HILE** Vicki dozed, Lionel listened to Zeke and Mac talk about the different disguises the group in Petra might need for an upcoming mission. Zeke said he had found a book detailing new techniques for makeup, scars, skin and eye color, and blemishes.

Lionel was sad to leave Wisconsin, but he had been on the run so much in the past few years that this didn't feel much different. Though he loved his new friends in Wisconsin, he hadn't been there long enough to set down roots like Vicki had.

Lionel pulled out the sheet of paper Marshall had given him and read through the different messages. Some were printed from the computer, others handwritten. The one from Charlie, scrawled in pencil and slanting down one page, choked him up the most.

Dear Lionel,

I'm really sorry about your arm and have been praying for you since the accident. I hope the one Zeke made for you works good. I haven't known you as long as I've known Vicki and some of the others, but I want you to know that I've seen Jesus in you. You're always thinking of others and not yourself, always keeping people on track, and treating people like I imagine Jesus would.

I know Jesus wasn't black or anything, but I think you know what I mean. That's all I have to say. Thanks for being my friend.

Charlie

Lionel folded the page and smiled. Charlie's line about Jesus not being black reminded him how much he had been through since the disappearances. At first, Lionel felt uneasy being the only black teenager in the group, but with the earthquake and all the plagues and death around them, his skin color wasn't an issue. They were all believers in Christ. Period.

It was what Lionel imagined an army went through. He had read stories about soldiers who disliked others because of their differences. But once the bullets started to fly, it didn't matter where the people came from or how they talked or what they looked like—they were fellow soldiers.

Lionel heard Mac say something about Carpathia's ten kings, and he began listening again.

". . . 'course, he calls 'em regional potentates, but we know what's going down, don't we?" Mac said.

"I do," Zeke said.

Mac stretched his arms. "If Otto succeeds in New Babylon, we find out where the big shindig is gonna be before it happens, and we get in there and bug the place. We're not going to try to stop prophesied events, of course, but it'll be good to know exactly what's happening."

"What happens to Carpathia's secretary?"

Lionel had wondered about this as well. That Rayford had befriended a secretary working for Carpathia was one thing. But trusting her? Lionel thought it was risky but didn't say anything.

"Krystall?" Mac said. "If I had a vote, I'd say we convince her we know what's going to happen to New Babylon and get her out of there."

"To Petra?"

Mac shook his head. "Much as we might like to do that, God has set that city aside as a city of refuge for his people only. Sad as it is, she made her decision, took her stand, and accepted the mark. Getting her out of New Babylon just keeps her from dying in that mess when God finally judges the city. She's going to die anyway, sometime between then and the Glorious Appearing, and when she does, she's not going to like what eternal life looks like."

Lionel thought of all the people he had come into contact with during the last six years who fit into that category—people who had heard the truth but decided not to believe it. Some had chosen to take Carpathia's mark. Others were still out there who hadn't chosen, but that number was dwindling every day.

He closed his eyes and prayed for the San Diego group to get out safely. He asked God to help Buck and little Kenny and prayed that the Tribulation Force would be able to rescue Chloe. "And if they aren't able to rescue her, I pray you would give her the strength to go through whatever she's going to face.

"And, God, whatever you have for me in Petra—whether it's reaching out to people over the Internet, encouraging others, or

something else—I want to do it with everything in me."

✸

Judd awoke early and, using Otto's computer, accessed the many Global Community
news feeds. He came upon one from the
United North American States that disturbed
him.

A female reporter stood near a large
prison. "This courtyard here in Louisiana is
used for two purposes. Three times each day
prisoners are taken past the bronze statue of
Lord Carpathia so they can worship. And to
my right—" the camera panned—"are the
loyalty enforcement facilitators. Everyone
knows what those are used for."

Judd counted seven guillotines standing
like evil guards. The GC had televised executions for a long time, so he didn't understand
why the reporter was giving this background.
A black SUV pulled into the courtyard and a
handcuffed Chloe Williams was dragged out
of the vehicle, her head banging the door.

The reporter continued talking and moved
toward a group of media members. When
the camera panned back to Chloe, one of the
Global Community officials whirled and hit
her in the forehead with the back of his

hand. Then the man clamped his hand over her mouth, kneed her in the back, and tried to tape her mouth.

Chloe broke free for a moment and screamed, "Tell the truth for once! I was drugged! They—"

The man slapped the tape on her face so tightly that Judd wondered if Chloe could even breathe, let alone speak. Seeing someone he knew treated this way made Judd sick.

The reporter yelled at the GC officials, "Has she spilled any more?"

"Oh yes," the man said as Chloe shook her head. "More all the time. Of course we had to tell her there would be no trading leniency for, ah, physical favors as it were. She can only help herself by telling the truth. I'm confident we'll get there. We've already gained more knowledge about the Judah-ite underground and the illegal black-market co-op from her than from any other source we've ever had."

The man concluded by saying the daily executions would be held at 10 a.m. the next day with more than thirty executions lined up.

The camera panned back to the reporter. "Here in Louisiana prisons are notoriously hard, and none harder than Angola. International terrorist Chloe Williams will rue the day she pushed the Global Community to the point where she was sent here. The guillotine will be sweet relief compared to hard labor for the rest of her life." With a look of glee the reporter ended with, "When the life of this dissident comes to an end, we will show it to you here live."

Judd switched off the feed and buried his head in his hands. Someone touched him on the shoulder and Judd looked up.

"I'm sorry about your friend in America," Otto said. "We are all praying for her. I have an important mission this morning that may help the Trib Force find her. It's dangerous though. I have to go to the palace. Do you want to go with me?"

※

After seeing the GC coverage of Chloe Williams, Mark sent an urgent message to the Young Tribulation Force around the world, asking everyone to pray for Chloe, her family, and her friends. *And keep looking for anyone who may not have taken the mark of Carpathia.*

Everyone gathered in the main cabin in Wisconsin and prayed. Janie asked God to keep Chloe from giving any information that might hurt the Tribulation Force. Conrad prayed that no one would be captured in the rescue attempt, if there was one. Josey pulled her son to her chest and asked God to help little Kenny, who was without his mother.

Mark bit his lip. "And, God, whatever your will is, give us the courage to accept it."

※

Judd followed Otto closely as they crept into the palace of Nicolae Carpathia. It helped Judd to know that Nicolae and his top people were miles away in Al Hillah, but he still felt creepy walking the same halls and riding the same elevator as Nicolae and his aides.

There were no people in the halls. Somehow they had adjusted to the darkness and were trying to get back to work.

Otto pushed the button for the executive offices, and Judd rode the elevator up with him. Otto led him to the main office where Nicolae Carpathia's secretary, Krystall, sat talking on the phone.

"No, it's still painful, Mom," Krystall said. "I guess we're adjusting, but I can't do anything here except answer the phone. . . . No, they can evidently see fine in Al Hillah and don't have to follow his glow around anymore."

Otto pushed the door open slightly and it creaked.

Krystall sat up, her eyes wide. "I'm sorry, Mom. I need to go. Someone's here. Mmm-hmm. Bye."

"Krystall, don't be alarmed," Otto said. "I'm a friend of Rayford. I have a young man with me."

"What are you doing here?"

"I've been asked to speak to you."

"Is this about Rayford's daughter?" Krystall said.

"Yes, her location."

Krystall took a breath. "All I know is Angola Prison in Louisiana."

"Okay, I'll tell them. And the other thing is any information—"

The phone rang and Krystall jumped. "This might be the security chief, Akbar. He was supposed to call." She pointed a finger to the corner. "There's a phone over there if you want to listen."

Judd rushed to it and picked up as Krystall grabbed her own receiver. Judd held the receiver so Otto could hear too.

"This is Krystall."

"Krystall, Chief Akbar. Are you still in the dark there?"

"Yes, sir, as much as ever."

"All right. I have an update for you, if you'll take this down."

"Excuse me, sir, but how am I supposed to take it down?"

"Don't you have a system worked out yet? You could contact someone outside New Babylon and have them transcribe this message and send it out."

"Yes, sir, but—go ahead, I'll remember it."

"Good. Tell the ten heads of state that the government is up and running here in Al Hillah. We will not be deterred by these tricks of the enemy. They must know that we are in control of the situation."

"Yes, sir."

"Also, communicate to them that they should prepare for a meeting and celebration in Baghdad six months from now. Everyone is working on the preparations. The potentate wants this to be a great display with flags, banners, light shows. They have invited the singer Z-Van to be part of it, as well as other bands."

"This assumes the darkness will be gone—"

"If we figure out how to counteract this terrorist plot of darkness, we will all return to New Babylon. But no matter what happens, this meeting and celebration will take place in Baghdad."

"And where in Baghdad, may I ask?"

"At the new building—where the Iraq Museum used to be before the war."

"Yes, I know it."

"Everything will be first-class, state-of-the-art. The meetings at this venue will of course be closed, but the potentate wants some of the festivities open to the public. We'll have the media covering this as well, so we need to make accommodations for them."

"Yes, sir."

"And one more thing, Krystall. Make sure you communicate that at this meeting we will discuss the final solution to the Jewish problem."

Otto elbowed Judd and grimaced. When Krystall was finished, Otto thanked her for letting them listen. "Is there anything we can do for you?"

"Just leave quickly and quietly. I don't want anyone knowing you were here."

Otto's phone rang and he stepped into the hall.

Judd stayed in the office while Krystall fumbled through a desk drawer. "Can I help you find something?" he said.

Krystall jumped, then settled. "I'm looking for a voice recorder I had in the top drawer. I thought I'd record what I can remember of Suhail's message, then phone someone to transcribe it."

Judd moved behind the desk and quickly found the recorder.

Otto came back inside. "Krystall, one more question. Your information about Chloe Williams. Is that from inside knowledge or just from the news?"

"Both," Krystall said. "I did see the news-cast, but I also heard Security and Intelligence people talking about Chloe being there. The latest information I had was that she was to be executed at 1000 hours Central Time."

FIFTEEN

Last Words

VICKI awoke a couple of hours before they touched down in Petra, and Lionel caught her up on what he had heard from Mac and Zeke. "From what Mac says, it doesn't look good for Chloe."

"What about Judd?" Vicki said.

"If he's with this Otto guy, Mac's going to pick them up after we land in Petra."

Vicki nodded and breathed a silent prayer of thanks.

"There's something else," Lionel said. "I don't know if you picked this up from reading Scripture, but Mac said Tsion believes New Babylon is going to be destroyed."

Vicki thought of the passage in Revelation 18. It ended with the words: *"She will be utterly consumed by fire, for the Lord God who judges her is mighty."*

At 2 p.m. local time, Sam Goldberg met the plane and helped Zeke unload his things. Another Trib Force pilot, Abdullah Smith, had a bigger plane ready for Mac and came for Zeke.

Vicki turned to Mac before he left. "Be careful."

"You bet," Mac said. "Like I just told Zeke, I hope to get back here before the GCNN goes on the air with Chloe—assuming everything we've heard is true."

Sam took Vicki and Lionel into the camp. The sight of Petra took Vicki's breath away. The red rocks seemed to reach into the sky. And seeing a million people spread out in the camp, knowing they were all believers who had been protected by God, gave Vicki a feeling of safety she'd never felt.

"Lionel will stay with me," Sam said. "Vicki, you will have your own place."

"I don't need—"

"It's already been settled. I talked with Mr. Stein and he said Tsion and Dr. Rosenzweig want to see you, but after this thing with the American woman is settled."

"What have you heard about Chloe?" Vicki said.

"We think the Global Community is setting a trap for the Trib Force in a place called Louisiana. I overheard Chang and

Naomi talking earlier. Chang has the ability now to interfere with GC broadcasts."

"Are they going to televise Chloe's execution?" Vicki shuddered. It was a spectacle Vicki never wanted to see, but if her sister in Christ was going to be killed, Vicki wanted to witness the woman's last moments on earth.

As they walked farther, a robed figure walked toward them, the sun at his back. When they got closer, Vicki recognized Mr. Stein and hugged him.

"We've prayed for you for so long," Mr. Stein said, "and now you're here."

Vicki nodded. "Now we should pray for Judd."

Judd stood at a secluded spot near the New Babylon runway with about thirty other believers from Otto's group. Zvi had become so scared he would be arrested that he, Westin, Gunther, and some others decided to take their chances driving a school bus through the desert. Before they had left, Westin shook hands with Judd and smiled. "Hope I can attend your wedding at Petra, but if not, I'll be thinking about you."

Otto was now back at the palace for one

last trip. As the plane circled for a landing, Otto returned, his face white.

"What's wrong?" Judd said.

"I went to thank Krystall for her help and found her body."

"She's dead? What happened?"

"I don't know. She was on the floor and the phone was buzzing. Perhaps the GC found out she was giving us information."

Judd shook his head. "Sounds like something Carpathia would do." He looked around at the sidewalks and doorways of the airport. There were dead bodies lying around. Some people were still alive, and Judd wanted to help them. They called out for food or water.

"I've got a question," Judd said. "Wasn't there supposed to be an angel or something that warned us to get out of here?"

"I guess it hasn't occurred yet," Otto said.

"Which means there must be more believers here than us," Judd said.

Otto nodded. "Yes, there are some who elected not to go with us, so they will somehow need to get out of here with the help . . ."

The plane engines drowned out the rest of Otto's words. When the plane stopped and Mac let down the stairs, the people with Otto tried to individually thank Mac, but he tried to keep them moving up the stairs.

When Mac saw Judd, he grinned and slapped Judd's back. "I dropped off a redhead in Petra. Get on the plane, boy. I'm taking you home."

Judd couldn't help laughing as he got on the plane. As Mac and Otto spoke at the bottom of the stairs, a sense of peace came over him. During his stay in New Babylon, he hadn't let himself think of the next day. He simply survived minute by minute. Now his thoughts turned to Petra and who was waiting for him.

※

Vicki joined Lionel and hundreds of thousands at the huge video display on the side of a mountain. Sam Goldberg explained that they normally didn't watch executions, but Tsion had asked everyone to be in prayer for Chloe and believed they should show the coverage.

Vicki thought of Buck, Rayford, and Kenny and wondered if they were watching. Surely they wouldn't let the little boy see such a horrible sight.

When Vicki arrived, Chloe was being led through the gauntlet of reporters and the crowd. People cheered and clapped. The camera zoomed in on Chloe, and Vicki caught her breath. Even with the drab prison clothing she looked radiant.

The camera panned away, and Vicki noticed prisoners with the Star of David stenciled onto their clothes. These were Jews who had been starved, beaten, and tortured. They looked almost relieved to be nearing death.

The GC man in charge, Jock Ashmore, was introduced to the delight of the crowd. "We have thirty-six executions to carry out for you today," he said, "twenty-one for murder, ten for refusing to take the mark of loyalty, four for miscellaneous crimes against the state, and one for all those charges and many, many more."

The crowd went wild.

"I am happy to say that though Mrs. Chloe Steele Williams did not in the end agree to accept the mark of loyalty to our supreme potentate, she did provide us with enough detailed information on her counterparts throughout the world to help us virtually wipe out the Judah-ites outside of Petra and to put an end to the black-market co-op."

The crowd clapped and cheered again.

Vicki couldn't believe they were actually going to show all thirty-six executions live. All around her, people prayed softly. Some wept.

Vicki heard the screaming engines of a

plane and looked at Lionel. They both
jumped up and ran down the hill with Sam.

⁕

Judd was never happier to be back on the
ground than when he stepped off the plane
in Petra. As he helped the others find their
way to the narrow entrance to the ancient
city, he saw Sam, Lionel, and Vicki running
toward him.

"What are you waiting for?" Mac said. "Go
on!"

Judd waved as he ran, whooping and
hollering. Sam and Lionel slowed, and Vicki
reached Judd and threw her arms around
him. She put her lips close to Judd's ear, and
Judd could feel her hot tears on his face.

"You're back! You're finally back, and
we're never going to be separated again!"

"You got that right," Judd said. "From now
on, wherever I go, you go."

Judd ran alongside Vicki as Sam and
Lionel took the lead. Instead of going to the
big screen, Sam led them to the computer
center. Chang Wong stared at a computer,
and Naomi was behind him, her hands on
his shoulders.

Chang and Naomi welcomed them and
had them sit at a screen near the front. "The

elders and some others are together in the back," Chang said. "Did you hear about what just happened?"

"I just got here," Judd said.

"The head of this whatever you call it, Jock something, was about to execute ten people in a row who had refused to take the mark. But before he could . . ." Chang paused and clicked on a computer. "I'll show you."

While the main feed continued, Judd watched a replay of what had happened. Something bright appeared in the middle of the courtyard, and an angel towered over Jock and the others. Judd guessed the angel had to be at least fifteen feet tall. His clothes were so white the crowd had to shield their eyes.

The camera shook when the angel spoke. "I come in the name of the most high God," he began. "Hearken unto my voice and hear my words. Ignore me at your peril. 'Oh, that men would give thanks to the Lord for His goodness, and for His wonderful works to the children of men!'

"For He satisfies the longing soul and fills the hungry soul with goodness. You who sit in darkness and in the shadow of death are bound in affliction because you rebelled against the words of God and despised the counsel of the Most High.

"Cry out to the Lord in your trouble, and

he will save you out of your distress. He will bring you out of darkness and the shadow of death and break your chains in pieces.

"Thus says the Son of the most high God: 'I am the resurrection and the life. He who believes in Me, though he may die, he shall live. And whoever lives and believes in Me shall never die.'

"But woe to you who do not heed my warning this day. Thus says the Lord: 'If anyone worships the beast and his image, and receives his mark on his forehead or on his hand, he himself shall also drink of the wine of the wrath of God, which is poured out full strength into the cup of His indignation. He shall be tormented with fire and brimstone in the presence of the holy angels and in the presence of the Lamb.

" 'And the smoke of their torment ascends forever and ever; and they have no rest day or night, who worship the beast and his image, and whoever receives the mark of his name.' "

"Incredible," Vicki said, as Chang switched back to the live feed.

"I was ready to pull Chloe's execution off the air, but this is too good," Chang said. "God is even using this terrible event to reach people."

Chang and Naomi excused themselves and moved farther into the bowels of the center. Judd wished he could talk with Tsion Ben-Judah, but he knew this wasn't the time or place.

"I don't get it," Vicki said. "If there's an angel there, surely he could rescue Chloe. It doesn't seem fair."

Sam shook his head. "Why have any of us been saved or rescued? God has helped us, but others he has allowed to go through the fire. Who can know God's purposes?"

Judd put an arm around Vicki. "And we have to trust him, no matter what happens to Chloe or to us."

Though the leader of the executions had tried to tell the crowd not to worry about the angel, calling it a trick, the people looked frightened.

A short while later the executions continued with the deaths of what looked like seven true believers being beheaded at once. But just as the blades were about to come down, the screen filled with such a bright light that no one could see.

"We will not be delayed by this trick of the enemy!" Jock said and counted to three. The heavy blades dropped, and the people cheered, but no one could see the actual beheadings.

For the next half hour, the schedule continued and it seemed the angel had vanished. Judd, Lionel, Vicki, and Sam joined hands and prayed for Chloe.

When the others had all been executed, Judd put an arm around Vicki. "You don't have to watch this."

"I know, but I feel like it's the least I can do for her."

Suddenly the angel appeared again and Chloe grabbed the microphone. "A famous martyr once said he regretted he had but one life to give," Chloe began softly. "That is how I feel today. On the cross, dying for the sins of the world, my own Savior, Jesus the Christ, prayed, 'Father, forgive them, for they do not know what they do.'

"My personal preference? My choice? I wish I could stay with my family, my loved ones, my friends, until the glorious appearing of Jesus, who is coming yet again. But if this is my lot, I accept it. I want to express my undying love to my husband and to my son. And eternal thanks to my father, who led me to Christ.

"A famous missionary statesman, eventually martyred, once wrote, 'He is no fool who gives what he cannot keep to gain what he cannot lose.' He was talking about his life on earth versus eternal life with God. In my flesh I do not look forward to a death the likes of which you have already witnessed thirty-five times here today. But to tell you the truth, in my spirit, I cannot wait. For to be absent from the body is to be present with the Lord. And as Jesus himself said to his Father at his own death, 'Into Your hands I commit My spirit.'

"And now, 'according to my earnest expectation and hope that in nothing I shall be ashamed, but with all boldness, as always, so now also Christ will be magnified in my body, whether by life or by death. For to me, to live is Christ, and to die is gain. . . . For I am hard pressed between the two, having a desire to depart and be with Christ, which is far better.'

"And to my compatriots in the cause of God around the world, I say, 'Let this mind be in you which was also in Christ Jesus, who, being in the form of God, did not consider it robbery to be equal with God, but made Himself of no reputation, taking the form of a bondservant, and coming in the likeness of men. And being found in appearance as a man, He humbled Himself and became obedient to the point of death, even the death of the cross.

"'Therefore God also has highly exalted

Him and given Him the name which is above every name, that at the name of Jesus every knee should bow, of those in heaven, and of those on earth, and of those under the earth, and that every tongue should confess that Jesus Christ is Lord, to the glory of God the Father.

" 'Now to Him who is able to do exceedingly abundantly above all that we ask or think, according to the power that works in us . . . and to present us faultless before the presence of His glory with exceeding joy, to God our Savior, who alone is wise, be glory and majesty, dominion and power, both now and forever.' "

Vicki wiped away a tear. Judd was holding her tightly with one arm and the other he had around Lionel's shoulder.

"Buck and our precious little one," Chloe continued, "know that I love you and that I will be waiting just inside the Eastern Gate."

Chloe put the microphone down and walked to one of the guillotines. The camera followed her slowly as she knelt and laid her head under the blade. Then a glow of white light shone so bright that no one saw the blade come down and end Chloe's life on earth.

SIXTEEN

Holding Kenny

THE first thing Vicki wanted to do after the broadcast was see Chloe's son, Kenny. She found him with Chang's sister, Ming Toy. Kenny came to Vicki right away, and she held him tightly for a long time. The boy was still asking where his mother was and when he would see her.

"Buck should be here tomorrow," Ming whispered to Vicki.

Kenny reached for Vicki's hand, and she sang him songs and helped him get to sleep that night, with the promise of exploring Petra in the morning.

When daylight came, Vicki, Judd, and Kenny walked along the rocks and watched the people gather manna.

Vicki could tell Judd was shocked by what had happened to Chloe, but they didn't want to talk about it in front of Kenny.

Later in the morning Kenny rode with Ming to meet the plane that touched down on the runway. A man staggered from the aircraft, grabbed Kenny, and held him tight. Vicki grabbed binoculars and saw it was his father, Buck.

Vicki ached to hear some kind of teaching from Tsion. She couldn't think of anything that would give more comfort than Dr. Ben-Judah, and she didn't have to wait long. As soon as Buck, Rayford, and the others reached the camp, Tsion called them all together.

Several hundred gathered at the high place, within the sound of rushing water from the stream. Zeke, Vicki, Lionel, and Judd stood with other friends from Illinois who had known Chloe personally. Kenny's arms were still wrapped around Buck's neck as Buck walked forward. When he saw Vicki and Judd, he managed a slight smile and touched her shoulder. Then he sat on a rock shelf and took in the scene.

Tsion held up his Bible and talked about his study of it the past few years. He said he could see God's fingerprints on every page. "I love this book! I love this Word! I love its author, and I love the Lord it represents. Why do I speak of the Word of God today when we have come with heavy, heavy hearts to remember two dear comrades and loved ones?

"Because both Albie and Chloe were people of the Word. Oh, how they loved God's love letter to them and to us! Albie would be the first to tell you he was not a scholar, hardly a reader. He was a man of street smarts, knowledgeable in the ways of the world, quick and shrewd and sharp. But whenever the occasion arose when he could sit under the teaching of the Bible, he took notes, he asked questions, he drank it in. The Word of God was worked out in his life. It changed him. It helped mold him into the man he was the day he died.

"And Chloe, our dear sister and one of the original members of the tiny Tribulation Force that has grown so large today. Who could know her and not love her spirit, her mind, her spunk? What a wife and mother she was! Young yet brilliant, she grew the International Commodity Co-op into an enterprise that literally kept alive millions around the globe who refused the mark of Antichrist and lost their legal right to buy and sell.

"In various safe-house locations over the past half-dozen years, I lived in close proximity to Chloe and to her family. It was common to find her reading her Bible, memorizing verses, trying them out on people. Often she would hand me her Bible and ask me to check her to see if she had a verse correct, word for word. And she always wanted to know exactly what it meant. It was not enough to know the text; she wanted it to come alive in her heart and mind and life.

"To those who will miss Chloe the most, the deepest, and the most painfully until we see her again in glory, I give you the only counsel that kept me sane when my own beloved were so cruelly taken from me. Hold to God's unchanging hand. Cling to his Word. Fall in love with the Word of God anew. Grasp his promises like a puppy sinks its teeth into your pant legs, and never let go.

"Buck, Kenny, Rayford, we do not understand. We cannot. We are finite beings. The Scripture says knowledge is so fleeting that one day it will vanish. 'For we know in part and we prophesy in part. But when that which is perfect has come,' and oh, beloved, it is coming, 'then that which is in part will be done away.

" 'When I was a child, I spoke as a child, I understood as a child, I thought as a child; but when I became a man, I put away childish things. For now we see in a mirror, dimly, but then face to face.'

"Did you hear that promise? 'But then . . .' How we can rejoice in the *but then*s of God's

Word! The *then* is coming, dear ones! The *then* is coming."

Vicki wept through the rest of the service, thinking of Chloe and her family.

※

A few days later, Ming Toy and a pilot named Ree Woo were married. Not wanting to take away from the memorial service or Ming and Ree's wedding, Judd and Vicki spent a few more days waiting and preparing.

When the time came, Chang Wong linked by video with the group in Wisconsin so they could see the ceremony. Judd and Vicki had chosen a beautiful spot overlooking the spring of water. Everyone said Vicki looked lovely in her dress. When Vicki saw Judd, she tried to keep from crying but couldn't. She wished her family could have been there to share the moment. She wished she could have met Judd's mom and dad.

They had written their own vows and both wept openly as they read their words to each other. Tsion spoke for a few minutes and challenged both Judd and Vicki to give their love to each other and their lives to God. "We do not know exactly what the next year will bring, but my prayer for you is that you would both grow in the grace of our Lord, until he comes again."

As the ceremony ended, manna fell. For the first time, Judd showed Vicki the home he had prepared.

"It's not much, but it's ours," Judd said as he picked Vicki up and carried her into the small dwelling.

ABOUT THE AUTHORS

Jerry B. Jenkins (www.jerryjenkins.com) is the writer of the Left Behind series. He owns the Jerry B. Jenkins Christian Writers Guild, an organization dedicated to mentoring aspiring authors. Former vice president for publishing for the Moody Bible Institute of Chicago, he also served many years as editor of *Moody* magazine and is now Moody's writer-at-large.

His writing has appeared in publications as varied as *Reader's Digest*, *Parade*, *Guideposts*, in-flight magazines, and dozens of other periodicals. Jenkins's biographies include books with Billy Graham, Hank Aaron, Bill Gaither, Luis Palau, Walter Payton, Orel Hershiser, and Nolan Ryan, among many others. His books appear regularly on the *New York Times*, *USA Today*, *Wall Street Journal*, and *Publishers Weekly* best-seller lists.

Jerry is also the writer of the nationally syndicated sports story comic strip *Gil Thorp*, distributed to newspapers across the United States by Tribune Media Services.

Jerry and his wife, Dianna, live in Colorado and have three grown sons.

Dr. Tim LaHaye (www.timlahaye.com), who conceived the idea of fictionalizing an account of the Rapture and the Tribulation, is a noted author, minister, and nationally recognized speaker on Bible prophecy. He is the founder of both Tim LaHaye Ministries and The PreTrib Research Center. He also recently cofounded the Tim LaHaye School of Prophecy at Liberty University. Presently Dr. LaHaye speaks at many of the major Bible prophecy conferences in the U.S. and Canada, where his current prophecy books are very popular.

Dr. LaHaye holds a doctor of ministry degree from Western Theological Seminary and a doctor of literature degree from Liberty University. For twenty-five years he pastored one of the nation's outstanding churches in San Diego, which grew to three locations. It was during that time that he founded two accredited Christian high schools, a Christian school system of ten schools, and Christian Heritage College.

Dr. LaHaye has written over forty books that have been published in more than thirty languages. He has written books on a wide variety of subjects, such as family life, temperaments, and Bible prophecy. His current fiction works, the Left Behind series, written with Jerry B. Jenkins, continue to appear on the best-seller lists of the Christian Booksellers Association, *Publishers Weekly*, *Wall Street Journal*, *USA Today*, and the *New York Times*.

He is the father of four grown children and grandfather of nine. Snow skiing, waterskiing, motorcycling, golfing, vacationing with family, and jogging are among his leisure activities.

The Future Is Clear

Check out the exciting Left Behind: The Kids series

#1: The Vanishings

#2: Second Chance

#3: Through the Flames

#4: Facing the Future

#5: Nicolae High

#6: The Underground

#7: Busted!

#8: Death Strike

#9: The Search

#10: On the Run

#11: Into the Storm

#12: Earthquake!

#13: The Showdown

#14: Judgment Day

#15: Battling the Commander

#16: Fire from Heaven

#17: Terror in the Stadium

#18: Darkening Skies

#19: Attack of Apollyon

#20: A Dangerous Plan

#21: Secrets of New Babylon

#22: Escape from New Babylon

#23: Horsemen of Terror

#24: Uplink from the Underground

#25: Death at the Gala

#26: The Beast Arises

#27: Wildfire!

#28: The Mark of the Beast

#29: Breakout!

#30: Murder in the Holy Place

#31: Escape to Masada

#32: War of the Dragon

#33: Attack on Petra

#34: Bounty Hunters

#35: The Rise of False Messiahs

#36: Ominous Choices

#37: Heat Wave

#38: The Perils of Love

BOOKS #39 AND #40 COMING SOON!

www.leftbehind.com

Hooked on the exciting
Left Behind: The Kids series?
Then you'll love the dramatic audios!

Listen as the characters come to life in this theatrical
audio that makes the saga of those left behind
even more exciting.

High-tech sound effects, original music,
and professional actors will have you
on the edge of your seat.

Experience the heart-stopping action and
suspense of the end times for yourself!

Five exciting volumes available on CD or cassette.

Hooked on the exciting
Left Behind: The Kids series?
Then you'll love the dramatic audios!

Listen as the characters come to life in this theatrical
audio that makes the saga of those left behind
even more exciting.

High-tech sound effects, original music,
and professional actors will have you
on the edge of your seat.

Experience the heart-stopping action and suspense of the end times for yourself!

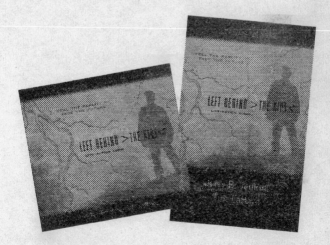

Five exciting volumes available on CD or cassette.